GRAY HEARTS

-AND-

GREENBACKS

A NOVEL

BY

WILLIAM BRENNAN

In memory of
Henry F. Sullivan
My uncle, patron and hero

ONE

My name is Tommy Phelan and my tale begins in the spring of 2005 when it was all hands on deck for the viewing of the body.

Now I don't like wakes anymore than the next guy but my boss, Fred Callahan, had been killed by a hit and run driver so the troops had better damn well all be there suggestion was issued to the members of the Corps of Engineers contracting office at Ft. Belvoir.

Would you believe that the poor bastard was being laid out on St. Patrick's Day? I'd say that it was damn shitty form to knock off an Irishman at a time when he'd have to be waked on our patron saint's day. True to the season, it couldn't have been a more miserable night with strong Alberta winds driving ice water bee-bees into the faces of the already morose mourners as they walked from the parking lot to the Fairfax Memorial Funeral Home.

I was about fifth or sixth in the receiving line and had no idea what the hell I was supposed to say to the widow, but given the moaning emanating from up ahead, some of those preceding me had obviously pressed some of the poor woman's most sensitive buttons.

To tell you the truth, I didn't know Fred very well, being relatively new to his branch – just under six months. We'd never had what you'd call a real personal conversation in that time, but the man had always been nice to me – he had.

That was it; he was very kind to me. Thank the Lord! It was my 'eureka' moment and my theme for the spectacle in progress.

I lucked out and was lined up behind our division director John Barrow and took comfort in thinking that I might be able to take a few cues from his performance.

The closer I got to the family, the more the wailing and weeping up ahead at ground zero ate at my innards. Callahan's death was a shock to all and since it was somewhat related to work and therefore a kind of an in-the-line-of- duty loss, the employees of the office of contracts had been nudged to pay their respects – not that the push had been hard or needed. As far as I could tell, Fred had always treated his employees well; I never saw any signs that he bullied anyone in the few months that I worked for him, so I was convinced that the tears were legit.

Oh God, as I peered into my near future I could see Barrow's wife and the widow were locked up in an embrace and were swaying like willows in the face of a hurricane with all of the accompanying sound and water works. I couldn't make out what they were saying but there could be no doubt about their pain.

As the line scrunched up waiting for the women to tear themselves apart, Barrow turned to me and, under his breath, coughed and said, "Not such a great day for the Irish, eh Phelan?"

"You got that right," I replied and opined inwardly that March is not a good month to die. Nasty cold rain, I wouldn't want to be put down in this kind of weather. A beautiful day in May's more my style – maybe Kentucky Derby Saturday with all the good looking girls wearing lovely, colorful, broad brimmed hats and mourning poor Tommy with beautiful roses and mint juleps at the ready - but don't get me wrong, I'm not bucking for a quick exit.

The pressure in the line continued to grow and I watched as the women wrenched themselves apart and John moved to embrace the still slobbering widow. "God, Mil, I'm so sorry. For more than twenty-five years Fred was my best friend both in the office and life itself. I feel terrible that I asked him to stay late to help with a project. If only we'd quit a couple of minutes earlier or later, he'd still be with us. And it was my fault that I suggested that we stop for a beer, just one to help us wind down. The last thing he said to me as we walked out of the bar was, `I'll see you in the morning.'"

The widow sagged more heavily as Barrow moved even closer to provide greater support and continued, "The next thing I remember was standing over him in the middle of the highway. There was no doubt in my mind that he was gone, but I was certain that he never felt a thing. Gradually, I woke up to the fact that the police were trying to question me, and I couldn't decipher a word they were saying; when I pieced it together, Fred was dead and there was no car and no driver, nothing but me standing helplessly as the police surveyed the scene."

The widow was racked with spasms as Barrow continued, "I felt responsible that night, Mil, and I still do."

By this point she was wailing uncontrollably, but between her wracking sobs she blurted, "You had nothing to do with it, John, really don't blame yourself."

The process became surreal. I moved to the head of the line, "I'm very sorry or your loss, Mrs. Callahan. I worked for Fred for only a short time, but he was always very kind to me and to all of his employees." I barely recognized my voice. It was as if another person had said the paltry lines, and I pushed on through the gauntlet of the victim's adult children toward the bier.

I did my damndest to focus on the shiny metal casket rather than on the heavily made up corpse. All I could think about as I viewed the remains was that the whole scene was nothing but bullshit. He got blasted; just close the damn lid on him. When I got a closer look at the box, I was amazed. It was one hell of a vehicle to the hereafter, a friggin' space ship that obviously cost a damn fortune; the Callahans must have some major league dough. But they ain't sending the poor bastard to the moon. In the morning, they'll be putting him on a cart and dropping him in a hole out back of here.

Psychologically drained, I took one last somber look at the corpse; it was simply an object and I spent only enough time to try to convince others that I, too, was in deep mourning before moving to a seat away from the Barrows and the other members of the staff who had gravitated to the back of the huge viewing room. While sitting there I made a vow: 'Here today, gone tomorrow. Fred Callahan you were always nice to me and I'll try to remember you.'

Checking my watch after thirty mind numbing minutes, I slipped out into the bleak night without talking to anyone or taking leave of the family.

TWO

"Tommy! Tommy Phelan? It is you!" The willowy honey blond appeared nonplussed at coming upon me in Brennan's Restaurant in the French Quarter of New Orleans.

My jaw dropped; it had been more than eleven years since high school and I hadn't laid eyes on Amanda Swenson even once in the interim. Trying to avoid being too obvious, I gave her an indirect survey and confirmed that she remained the best looking – and best put together – woman that I'd ever known.

Attempting to gain my composure, I took a second to pat my mouth with the rich linen napkin all the while staggering to my feet and stammering, "Wow! Ah... You're the...ah last person I expected to see...ah... I mean...here in New Orleans."

Turning to my boss, who had already risen, I said, "John, this is...ah,..Amanda Swenson, a classmate of mine at West Springfield High School."

"Amanda, this is my boss, John Barrow."

Barrow, being very cool, nodded and said, "Very nice to meet you, Amanda. Do you still live in Northern Virginia?"

"My pleasure, Mr. Barrow."

Turning to me she lectured, "But it's not Swenson, Tommy; surely you remember that I married Matt Roby."

Back to John, she smiled and assured him, "And yes, I live in McLean."

Throwing up my hands and raising my eyebrows as a confession of utter failure, I said, "Of course, but I haven't seen you since graduation and that was ninety-four and… you know, old habits die hard."

Barrow covered his mouth and coughed before being able to interject, "We're just finishing breakfast. Would you care to join us for coffee, Amanda?"

"I'd love to, but I'm already late for a meeting with old college friends in the rear. We're among the last of the real Sophie Newcombs so we're required to show up in support of the cause of the day, whatever it happens to be, and I'm not sure what today's crisis is...never know," she said with self deprecating charm.

Facing me, she flashed a spectacular smile and asked, "Where are you staying, Tommy? I'll give you a call if you're going to be in town this evening."

"We're at the Holiday Inn on...um... Royal. I'm… I'm here till tomorrow...yeah I'd like to catch up." My stammering was getting worse, and I realized that it was becoming an embarrassment to both Amanda and Barrow who were averting their eyes as I struggled, and I felt myself flush from the pressure.

With another warm smile and a slight perky nod to each of us, Amanda turned and followed the hostess who had been waiting at a discreet distance to escort her to join her friends.

As we sat, John said, "Wow! What a looker! She could be in Hollywood."

Gathering myself, I said, "You know it. She was gorgeous when we were in high school but she's even more smashing now. I'm sorry I couldn't talk; that was a shock seeing her here."

"No wonder you were tongue tied."

I laughed. "Yeah, she always had instant access to my stammer button."

"You were after her?"

After a real belly-laugh, I said, "Yeah, you could say that. The football team, the band, the glee club - all were around her locker like flies around spilled honey.

"And I was usually pretty far back in the fly flock," I added with another guffaw.

Changing gears, John coughed spasmodically as he tried to laugh and said, "I already hate myself, but it's a `swarm'.

"What?"

"Nothing; let it go," he mumbled under his breath.

"By the way, breakfast is on me. It's way over the Corp's per diem rate, and I wanted to show you how the other half dines in the capital of Cajun Country.

"We're not due in class for more than an hour, but I have to go to the office to check on what's happening back at the ranch so I'll leave you on your own. I'll see you in class."

"Yeah; thanks, John, I appreciate it. Wow! Brennan's! I've heard about it for years; it was a real treat."

Still perplexed, I asked, "Before I forget, what's a Sophie Newsom? You seemed to get Amanda's point."

"A `Sophie Newcomb,'" he corrected, "It's the women's college of Tulane University here in New Orleans. I don't know much about it, but if I remember correctly, it was pretty much a goner in the wake of Hurricane Katrina. I think that's what she was saying in shorthand."

"That makes a little more sense now...I think."

The waiter came and I watched Barrow discreetly slip a crisp new hundred dollar bill into the rich leather folder. It was collected and quickly returned by the efficient server, and John left a twenty in the folder for the tip.

Outside, Barrow lit a cigarette and said, "See you in a bit."

As John continued to hack and shake and was unable to take even a single drag before departing with a shaky wave of his right hand, I watched in horror and thought, 'Better lay off of those butts…You're half friggin' dead.'

THREE

Waltzing into my hotel room after class, I saw immediately that the light on the phone cradle was flashing. "You're shittin' me," I mouthed and raced to pick up the receiver.

"Hi, Tommy, it's me, Amanda. Surprise, huh? It's ten thirty and we just finished our meeting and a few of us are going shopping. But I'll definitely be free after five. I'm staying at the Omni Royal Orleans on St. Louis St. Why don't you come by for a drink after work? I'd love to catch up. I don't have the number with me but just come on by when you're done. See you."

Her voice sparkled just as it did when we were in high school, and after the little man in my head whispered 'no' to no effect, he shouted, `No friggin' way, jackass; let this go. Know when to walk away and when to run. It's sprint time in the Olympics, baby; so just cool it here and catch your plane in the morning.'

My second thought was that it was high time for a cold shower so I could comply with the instructions of my leprechaun.

An hour later, I checked my watch and sauntered past the Royal Orleans for the fourth time while still arguing with my little man. Finally I stopped at the entrance and squared my shoulders. "Shit! You knew you were going in when you saw the blinking light so cut the crap," I chastised myself softly, and strode forcefully into the lobby.

Obtaining the number from the desk, I dialed the house phone without hesitating and without more mind games.

The voice purred, "I knew you'd come. We could always count on Mr. Reliable. Come right on up."

My little man and I listened to my lame assent with accompanying stammers. Damn, it could have been '94. I checked my jacket. Reaching for the elevator button, I hesitated before forcing myself to short arm the call button and whispered, "It's a little late for this."

The door to Amanda's suite was swung wide open; I knocked hesitantly on the frame and asked, "Anybody home?"

From the other room of what was obviously a suite, she glided toward me, a vision in a tan chemise that only hinted at the form swaying within it. The smile was radiant as she embraced me and planted a very, very light peck on my cheek and exclaimed, "I was thrilled to see you this morning.

"I can't believe that it's been more than ten years. We missed you at the reunion. It was great to see everyone, but I was sorry you weren't among them." Releasing me, she stepped back to survey the damage. "You look great, Tommy, even more handsome than when I last saw you. You're married," she said glancing at my left hand.

Angst rising, I unsuccessfully failed to avoid curling my hand away from her view and replied, "Yeah, and I have a daughter and a little boy and another baby on the way." How damn defensive and lame was that? I then compounded my felony with, "That's kind of why we weren't able to make the reunion."

"Of course, but I still wish you'd come.

"In any event, that's great; marriage becomes you. What's your wife's name?" she asked, the congenial smile never wavering.

"Jenifer…Jen Ryan; you remember her, she was a year after us."

"Jen, no fooling? I remember her very well. She was very nice…and very cute. You're a lucky man, Tommy. And two kids with another on the way; that is so awesome. Obviously, it agrees with you. I'm happy for both of you."

Suddenly feeling great relief that my over the top speculation on why I had been summoned to her room was off base, I said, "What about you? You and Matt have kids?"

The smile faded under the question's quickly gathering storm cloud, "Not yet. We try - but no luck…yet. Our lives have been blessed in so many other ways, but no…none yet," her voice trailed off as the sentence ended.

Noting the dimming of the light in her eyes, I hastily changed the subject. "You're doing well; a suite no less." Looking around at the rich appointments, I added, "Talk about awesome. These are mighty fancy digs. I heard that Matt struck gold; that you guys were off the charts and…"

Brightening again, she interrupted, "It's old, but it's the most charming hotel in the French Quarter. There are more modern places in town with more stars, but we love to stay here when we're in town.

"And yes it's been a magical ride. Two kids from Springfield – just magical."

"Yeah, I've heard over the years that Matt's made it big. That… "

"I said that we'd been blessed, but this isn't about Matt and me; it's about you, Tommy. I want to learn all about you…and Jen."

She touched my arm lightly to guide me onto the open balcony; her power was still electric, and I swear the hair on the spot jumped to attention. Stepping out, she directed my eyes on a visual survey of the old French Quarter that unfolded below us on the steamy late April evening. "It's a wonderland." she said.

"I've never seen anything like it," I said while unsuccessfully trying to identify landmarks. All the way to the Mississippi and north and south the famous old quarter that I'd only read about came alive. It was too early for the nightclubs to shine their bright lights, but the rich antebellum townhomes and the Creole cottages cooled by thick blankets of ivy were more than enough to thrill me. "I'm glad that I signed up for the course. I never dreamed that it was so beautiful or that I'd ever get the chance to see it up close like this. "You come here often?"

"Not as often as we'd like. We travel a lot for Matt's work, so New Orleans just doesn't get the attention we'd... or at least I'd like to give it. That's what made running into you so special."

After one last survey of the scene below, we retreated from the balcony, and she said, "How about a drink before dinner?" which, of course, left me virtually no option other than to remain, not that I tried hard to gin one up.

Drawing out an already tapped bottle of Chivas Regal from the liquor cabinet, she handed it to me, "Will this do?" she asked with her smile back at its brightest.

I could see saw that there would be hell to pay if I turned down her invitation to dinner but steeled myself for that moment, in hopes that I could. "You bet," I said with a jaw clenching grin.

She turned conspiratorial. "I don't normally brag, but Matt and I spent two weeks in Scotland playing golf and visiting distilleries."

"You do get around. The best I can say is that I visited the Budweiser brewery in Williamsburg a few years back, and played the Greendale municipal golf course in Franconia twice last summer."

She laughed. "I had that coming, but I wasn't consciously trying to one up you, truly."

I smiled and poured the Scotch into heavy tumblers that she drew from the refrigerator and which she had already pre-loaded with ice. Handing her one, I toasted, "To Scotland and golf!"

She retorted, "To our meeting and to many more with Jen and Matt!"

The Scotch went down like silk. "This is really fine stuff – way better than I'm used to."

"So tell me about this school that brings you to New Orleans," she said looking at me with an earnest and believing cast to her face.

`God she's good,' I thought, `She's acting like she really gives a shit.' "I work for the government – the Army Corps of Engineers back home in Virginia. They're big down here on the river, and they run lots of training programs for us. I'm a contracting officer, so I'm taking one on advanced contracting procedures." I was relaxing and noted that there was no longer even a hint of a stammer in my speech.

"John... Mr. Barrow, my boss, is one of the presenters."

"It sounds like you're doing very well, Tommy. I'm impressed.

"Where do you and Jen live?"

It was a batting practice pitch and I brightened. "Last month we moved into our new house in Kings Park West off of Braddock Rd., one of those small ranch houses up off of the high end of Commonwealth Boulevard."

"You really are getting ahead. So your kids will be going to West Springfield just like Mom and Dad."

"No, no…We're practically on the Robinson High School campus just outside of Fairfax City just across Braddock Road from George Mason University, so there'll be no dynasty at Springfield," I said with an attempt at a wry chuckle.

"Oh, yeah, now I remember; that's a very nice neighborhood," she said.

With no hesitation between subjects, she continued, "I have a reservation for dinner downstairs in five minutes and you're my escort."

Before I could refuse, she interjected, "I won't take no for an answer. You'd never let a poor girl far from home dine alone, would you? Of course not; besides their Rib Room is world famous; I guarantee that you'll love it."

"But…"

"No `buts'. Tonight you're my protector in chief."

FOUR

As I hauled my clubs out of the trunk, wouldn't you know my playing partner and buddy Jimmy Frawley slid into the parking space next to mine at the Greendale Golf Course in Franconia.

As the door of his car opened and Frawley began to emerge like a chick from a newly cracked egg, I commenced the ritual, "How're you doing, pal? Before we start, just for today, how about we pledge to avoid trash talk? While there ain't no doubt that I'm going to whip your useless ass, I promise not to mention your total incompetence at the game but to only state facts as they become evident…to all."

"Deal! Except for a few serious medical problems, I'm doing OK. I hear that you've been living on the Burke Lake driving range. I wanted to practice but my back's been killing me all winter. It hurts so much when I bend, I may have to ask you to tee up my ball, but don't jump if I accidently goose you; my nerves have been acting up. But I'm gonna do my absolute best under the circumstances," Jimmy said as he moved to shake hands. "I don't ever remember you beating me even with a spot, but with my back – and this being my first round of the year I'm going to need at least five strokes on each side."

"I thought that as an officer of the court you were obligated to at least be in the neighborhood of the truth with your statements."

"Shows what you know about the law. You better stick with addition and subtraction. You can do all four functions of math now? Long division was always your stumbling block – but you do have that down now …right? "

After a couple of additional insults, I changed the subject, "Before I forget, after we pay, remind me to tell you about my trip to New Orleans and who I ran into. You won't believe it."

"Tell me now."

"You have to be sitting in the cart."

We continued our trash talk through the check in and pay to play process with Frawley continually demanding that the intelligence be forthcoming, "Come on, Asshole, out with it."

"When you're in the cart…and holding on."

After we loaded the bags onto the cart, Frawley drove to the `in the hole' position to wait our turn on the tee and we greeted the two old guys we'd been teamed with.

You know how it is with municipal courses; it was given names only, so Bill and Dick would be playing with Jim and Tom. And, naturally, the seniors would be walking; young men find no benefit in strolling around a golf course and have little regard for money even when short of the commodity.

Watching the old timers warm up and hearing all the snapping and cracking of tendons and ligaments, I said quietly, "Both of 'em are at least a hundred. If one of them croaks on the course, I'm playing on. I'm not paying to run my own private ambulance service."

"Easy on that ambulance shit; don't forget, I chase 'em for a living. But it really does look like they can't make it. Maybe we should offer them a friendly bet, say ten bucks a hole?" Jim said with a hearty laugh that had to have been overheard.

"OK, spill it."

"Hold on to your seat. My boss and I are having breakfast – Eggs Benedict and all the fixings - in the fanciest place in New Orleans when this beautiful babe comes sashaying over and says loud enough for everyone in the whole place to hear, 'Tommy Phelan, I still love you, baby.' Guess who?"

"Alright bullshit artist, I'll bite; who?"

"Amanda Swenson looking ten times better than when we knew her, if that's humanly possible."

"No way!"

"Way! Seems she went to Tulane and was back in town for some sort of college sorority bullshit. But she goes gaga over me:` Tommy, Tommy, Tommy, remember when you used to hang around my locker just to sniff my ass?' `I do, I do.'"

"She really stopped and talked?"

"Really! You knew that she married Matt Roby and…"

"That jackass? Yeah, I remember him. Who the fuck doesn't?"

"You should! That jackass who, unlike you, practices real law and makes real money at it cut my ass out of that fine filly when we were sophomores."

"Sure, but we went three and six with him at quarterback. What a freakin' loser! But cut the crap; what happened?"

"My recollection was six and three, but I'm not a lawyer and not nearly as envious in my memory of dear old Matt. Besides, you were his primary receiver, so any lack of performance reflects just as badly on you."

Before I could go on, we were up on the tee. The sky was cobalt blue like the innards of the glaciers I saw in Alaska years back when I was a kid pulling my time in the National Guard. As a cumulous cloud formation in the south drifted away from us at flank speed, I tried to make nice with the old farts, "Great day, eh, guys? Looks like we can hit; they look halfway safe up behind the trees," I said as the foursome ahead of us turned the corner of the dog leg, right, on the first hole.

"You guys playing the yellow? We'll be playing white, if that's OK," Jim offered. The whites being the regular men's tees and the yellow the senior tees which are much closer to the greens – on most holes.

Dick reacted for the older set, "No, no…no. The whites are good with us. Show us the way, guys."

"Go ahead, Tommy. I have to take a couple of swings to loosen up."

I teed up and made my usual great practice swing and stepped up to the ball. Making what I thought was half way decent replica of what I'd just done, the ball sailed on a pretty good line toward the dog leg before fading into the tree line on the right. "Shit, can't anybody make a decent driver anymore? Damn, every club you buy these days is defective."

"That'll play," Jimmy piped in with false encouragement out of a sickly smirk as he prepared to hit. His mighty swing produced a short ground ball that dribbled off the end of the tee box.

"First round of the year," he said sheepishly. "I'm taking a Mulligan." The second ball took off to the right of center but duck-hooked back into the rough on the left, stopping just short of the drainage ditch. Head down, he stepped away in disgust and joined me in the cart to watch our senior citizens play.

Bill, the shorter and slighter, stepped up and hit a sweet line drive down the middle of the fairway about a hundred and eighty yards out. Dick placed a high fade around the dogleg about forty yards in front of mine and safely around the corner in position to be on the putting green with his second shot.

"God damn ringers; and you wanted to bet 'em?" I scolded Frawley.

"Well at least I didn't denigrate their ages. And remember, you called me to play, asshole."

As we drove to Jim's second ball, I said, "Screw golf. So where was I?... Oh, yeah; so Amanda, shaking and baking for me as I'm going gaga, actually invites me up to her hotel room for a drink after work, and..."

"And you finally banged her after all these fantasy filled but sexless years."

"Not exactly."

"Not fucking exactly; what the hell's that supposed to mean?"

"Well, if you need an exact word, NO...not yet, but she got to lamenting that her All American quarterback has been firing incompletions at her all these years and that they don't have any kids. So telepathically I sent her a message that I'd be glad to help."

"And?"

"We got interrupted and she forgot to return the message, but I'm sure it's coming.

"Hold on, Jimmy! I think the message is coming in as we speak."

"Phelan, you are one major league asshole."

Ignoring the fool's envy, I continued, "By the way, she must have spent fifteen minutes asking me how you were doing and all. When I told her that you were a lawyer like Mr. Touchdown, she started laughing. My earlier witticisms must have finally registered; certainly she wasn't guffawing at a favorite old classmate.

"Really, she couldn't get enough about you. Wanted to know who you married and…"

"You're shitting me?"

"How'd you know that? I asked her if she remembered you and she said, 'Who?'"

Shaking his head, Frawley said, "God, Phelan, you'll never change."

I roared.

We finished the hole. I took a seven and Jim picked up and said, "I lost count; put me down for a ten."

The honor to hit first went to Dick followed by Bill. As the round progressed, we, the younger set, began to laugh at our humiliation but soon a bit of good news was made known to those of us who actually work for a living: Bill and Dick would be dropping out after playing the first nine holes.

As we drove to the tenth tee, Jim said, "They were fading fast; we'd have had their decrepit asses on the back nine, easy."

As his ball hooked into the pond – following mine – and after a string of oaths that would have startled the crew of an aircraft carrier about his shot, Jim said, "So come on; finish up with the Amanda thing. What happened?"

"That was pretty much it. She really did invite me up for a drink and paid for my dinner. The bottom line was that she really seemed enthused about seeing me and the chance to catch up on things in Dogpatch."

"But of course. Did she really look that good?"

"Better than you can imagine: a ten plus; seriously."

By the time we got to the fourteenth hole, I had finish dropping all of my lies about Amanda and Matt and we settled down to golf until we took a pair of eights on the par three thirteenth hole.

We didn't even write down those scores and lamented that our cart had to be the slowest one on the lot. As we chased down our next drives, Jimmy asked, "Tommy, you got any money - real money? Or do you know where I can get some? A guy I know is trying to peddle me one of those small garden apartment projects up off of Little River Turnpike just before the Fairfax City line: two buildings, twenty-two units, eleven each. We're talking serious numbers, but almost all of it would be paper. All I have to raise is maybe a hundred thousand in cash. It's…"

"You're shittin' me, right? I can't even afford the green fees for this friggin' flood plain. Two and a half kids and a new mortgage and I'm supposed find a hundred thou for your fantasy real estate empire?"

"I mean it, Tommy. If I can find the dough, I can flip that project in a few months and pocket some real money. This market is taking off; I don't want to be left behind."

"Jim, boy, this bubble is going to burst like a nuclear blast over Baghdad. For the sake of your soul, I'll pray that you can't find the dough. That way I won't have to watch you bawl like a friggin' baby when I do your taxes next year."

"I'm serious, Phelan, there are fortunes to be made in real estate. We could do it. This guy has already flipped a bunch of apartments and has made a ton of dough."

"Listen up, moron; he wouldn't be hustling a bottom feeder like you, if he wasn't having trouble moving the friggin' thing. And, please, don't even think of dealing me in on this fiasco, so drop all the frigging' `wes'; singular `me' or `I' settles my stomach a lot better than the plural.

"Seriously, Jim, don't be in a hurry to get in. You can't afford it any more than I can, and this market's already been running too hot, too long. I think the shit's going to hit the fan. Keep your powder dry, baby.

"Do you have the numbers on occupancy and the rent receipts?"

"Yeah, I got it all."

"Tell you what; bring Nan and the kids over some night this week and I'll run 'em for you. In the meantime, don't do anything stupid."

That Wednesday evening as Jen and Nan supervised the children and sipped chardonnay, Jimmy and I disappeared down into the rec room to analyze the deal.

"Go get a couple of brews while I'm running these figures."

Jim went off to the basement refrigerator and returned with two cold ones. "Well?"

"I haven't even started on the numbers. But let me get this straight. You're thinking about giving a third mortgage on this dog?"

"That's right!" he said almost daring me to challenge the move.

So I did, "And you're a lawyer who's closed deals before?"

"So?"

"So you know where you'll stand if there is even a friggin' fart in the market?"

"Tom, get real; the market's headed nowhere but north. Sure, there'll be a bust someday… but not for a long time, five years, maybe longer. By that time, I'll have flipped this and three more projects and have a bundle of dough for my trouble."

"You actually believe that crap you're slinging?"

"I do; really; it's a friggin' gold rush"

"Wake up, moron! If this goes down while you're on the hook, you'll be in serious shit. You'll have as much chance of getting out of this mess as I have of winning the Mega Millions. But at least you'll be able to do your own bankruptcy filing.

"I don't have to waste running these numbers; just the summaries show how stupid it is. The rents barely cover the first mortgage. You'd be so far in the hole it would take spectacular growth to get you back to close to even, let alone way in the black. One broken window and you'll need a snorkel to get out from under water."

Jimmy responded with more than a little real hostility, "Don't you know anything? Are you so friggin' thick that you haven't seen that spectacular growth is exactly what's been happening."

"OK, OK, buy the fuckin' thing for all I give shit. You've been warned."

The mood suddenly went dark. "Tommy, do you like your job?"

"What's that supposed mean? It's OK, why?"

"Just try to imagine – if you can - how much I hate drawing up fuckin' wills? Going to court to challenge breathalyzer readings; challenging radar gun accuracy? Same old shit day after fucking day, listening to who hates who more in shitty marriages; same ol', same ol' every day.

"I don't know what I thought I was going to be doing at my age when I applied for law school, but I never dreamed it would be like this. I know I'm no world beater, but I thought I was a pretty smart kid, maybe not Supreme Court smart – at least not Chief Justice smart - but smart enough to tangle with pretty big boys. Man, I have to do something about this or I'll blow my friggin' brains out before I'm fifty."

Maybe it was the beer; whatever, he touched a nerve. "Yeah, I know. It's the same with me. In the government, we're all in lock step: in together, up and on together; out to pasture together; dead together.

"I know what you're up against; life sucks and then you die. I didn't mean to spit in your soup, but that project's a friggin' dog, Jimmy. I wish I could be more positive, and I'd sure like to start something with you, but this ain't the beginning of a real estate bubble; the needle to burst it has been launched."

We sat quietly and killed the two brews - and two more. I went into the basement and hauled in two more, and, slumped in our chairs, we chugged quickly and quietly.

Finally, I said, "Alright, asshole, upstairs for more trash talk and to convince the broads and the kids that we can't wait for tomorrow."

FIVE

Before I could get to the kitchen wall phone, Jen snatched it from its cradle. "Amanda, how nice to hear your voice...Yes, it has been a long time... Too long; right...Yes, he told me all about it...You know it, a huge coincidence."

She turned to me with an exaggerated turn of her head and twist of her hand. "Saturday? Why...yeah, yes I think we're... we're...um...free. Hold on! Let me get a pencil."

I grabbed a pencil from the counter and hustled it to her.

"Give me that again...Yes, I have it...seven o'clock.

"Nice talking to you too. See you then."

She hung up the phone with force great enough to make me wince and turned squaring her shoulders to face me. "I don't get it. We haven't seen or heard from this pair of climbers in a dozen years and all of a sudden we're the guests of honor at a party at their place – in McLean yet. What the hell's going on?"

I tried to act very casual, but my voice had a higher pitch than I was reaching for, "I don't know anything. It was a bolt from the blue...Hey, you're the one who accepted the invite, so let's just go with the flow. Once they show us their spread, that'll be the end of it. That way at the next reunion, we can vouch for their having made it big. It might not be anything more than that – really."

Walking away, she turned back quickly and said, "I'm not comfortable with this. I don't like it at all. We're not into social climbing; we're ordinary people."

I tried to take charge. "Damn it, don't start with me. I don't have a clue how it got this far. Let's just try to have a good time and stop looking for deeper meanings. But I'm as ignorant as you on the why. In school whenever I walked into their territory, they hit the road; now this?"

That Saturday evening as we pulled up in front of the Roby house, more accurately - mansion, I could tell from her squirming and repeated hand wringing that Jen was hot and getting ready to let me have a few more bars of her theme song, and almost immediately she was off to the races, "I told you that we weren't in this league, not with these people. Look at it, Tommy, it has to be worth a couple of million. God, it looks like they moved Monticello up here for the party, just for us. Good Lord, the wings are bigger than our whole house, and the field house at Robinson could fit inside the center."

My head was spinning, but she wouldn't relent so I interrupted her, "You said…"

She ploughed past with, "Can't we call in sick? They won't even know we didn't show. There have to be two dozen Mercedes, BMWs and Lexuses around the drive, and they're clean and shiny, real shiny. Look, even the damn tires sparkle.

"Look at the cars, Tommy; just in case you can't see, we're in our Malibu, the dingmobile with chipped paint and lots of rust spots." The sarcasm was dripping from her lips like so much bile, and I wondered why she wasn't oozing green slime. "They'll never even miss us. Let's just turn around…"

I cut her off with the hiss of a threatened viper, "We said – you said - we'd come. We have to go in. Really, Jen, knock this shit off. We don't ever have to come back, but we have to go in and make an appearance," the last sentence was spoken slowly and with as much intensity as I could manage, even as I kept the volume down. "Damn it, you know there's no way out. Now let's get our act straight and look like we belong."

Before she could react, I turned on her again. "No, get this: we do belong! We're as good as them any damn day. They're from Springfield, just like us. Because they fell into a bucket of shit and came up smelling like roses don't mean they're any smarter, harder working, more ambitious or any damn better. Maybe they're just luckier than…"

"Right, that's it; just a little luckier – about a million bucks more fortunate," she spat.

I heard the desperation and anger blend in my voice, "We're just as good as they are. They've got a few bucks more than us, is all."

Suddenly she pulled herself up straight in the seat. "OK, I'm in. I'm sorry. I'm going to suck it up, but I still think there's something really wrong here."

She turned to me and finished with, "Game, set, match! We shouldn't be here, but we are. I can handle it; let's go."

I implored her, "Can't you get it through your thick skull; these people can help us. They can. Now, are you ready to stop playing friggin' games and act like a god damn adult?"

She didn't say another word while unbuckling her seatbelt and opening the door. The sharp clicking of her heels on the paved walk sounded like small caliber gunfire; it told in no uncertain terms that she was still making me pay for some unknown or long forgotten sin as she stared straight ahead, accompanied by no one.

As we approached the house, I tried to be objective and saw that it wasn't nearly so over the top as Jen was describing it in her monologue for one. It was one of those hip roofed colonial revivals with wings on both sides that are fairly common in McLean and which resembled Monticello only in her blind with rage imagination. Hell, there wasn't a sign of a rotunda but I had to admit that it was pretty damn nice, maybe a million and a half bucks nice and probably worth four or five times as much as our ranch in Fairfax.

Climbing the three steps to the front entrance, I could see through the small vertical windows on the side of the massive oak door that the party was already in full swing.

"Don't you love the hand carved `R'? That we were at the Roby residence had completely slipped my mind," she offered in more smarm.

"Can't you see he's coming? For the love of God, let it go!" I begged.

The door swung open and Jen smiled like the rising sun and walked into the welcoming embrace that Matt Roby offered with exaggerated gestures.

"Jen, it's been way too long. Welcome to our home."

Before she could respond, he reached for my hand. "God, it can't be more than eleven years, Tommy. When Amanda told me that she'd had run into you in New Orleans, it touched off a host of memories – and ideas. We have to talk."

"Love to. Thanks for having us, Matt. You have a really magnificent place here. It's…"

I was interrupted by Amanda who bounded into an embrace with Jenifer. "I'm so glad you could make it, Jen, it's been ages."

Releasing her, Amanda turned to me and planted a light peck on my cheek. "Thanks for coming, Tommy. I really wanted you guys to come."

Matt grabbed my hand. "I understand that you're in contracting."

"Yeah," I puffed up, "with the Corps of Engineers."

Turning to Amanda, Matt said, "Hon, will you take Jen under your wing and show her around. I want a second with Tommy."

Without a skipped beat the two women disappeared into the noisy throng.

Holy mackerel, did I hear Roby right? A second with Tommy, good old Tommy? What the hell kind of parallel universe was he living in? When we were in high school good old Tommy was one of the untouchables.

Turning back to me, Roby took on a very serious cast. "You work on big projects? Construction?"

"Well, yeah, pretty big…I guess. All kinds of construction, yeah…sure. The Corps is big into heavy construction"

"We have to talk. One of the companies I represent has an interest in… is expanding and getting into big projects, and I don't have the expertise to deal with it. So…Oh, never mind, not now; it's party time. We'll get together another time - soon. Let's get you a drink and shelve this for later."

Two and half hours later, but still early, we made our good-byes and as Jen buckled her seat belt she said softly, "I'm sorry. I was horrible."

I had no doubt about her sincerity. "It's OK I had the jitters, too, and said more than a few things that I shouldn't have."

Turning onto Dolly Madison Boulevard and gaining speed on the way to the beltway and home, I felt the tension flow away in the slipstream of the dingmobile.

After another long silence, she broke the ice with, "I actually had a good time and met some nice people."

"Me too," I said with the welcome feeling that the tension was clearly heading in the right direction.

Her voice and tone were returning to normal, "We really are out of our league, but they treated me like I belonged. I had no idea that there were that many assistant secretaries in the government and that so many of them were women. And did you ever see more Eskimos? Jesus, Tommy, after a couple of wallops, I thought I had somehow wound up in Nome."

"Aside from the bullshit on the way in, I thought you said you weren't going to drink until the baby was born," I wasn't about to let that violation pass without comment.

She reacted negatively but without the white hot anger of the previous hours, "I wasn't but I really needed a couple to get with it. Let it go; will you? Mothers drank in the old days and most of us flourished – although I worry about you," she added with what I felt was a strained chuckle.

"Whatever. Anyway, from what little I could put together, Matt's practice is based on Eskimos and whatever they call the rest of those native people in Alaska, and somehow he's become a big shot by helping them out," I explained.

"That reminds me; what was your powwow with him about?" she asked.

"It never really developed, but I think he wants to hire me down the road. He's obviously got money up the wazoo and one of his companies is gearing up to develop some big construction jobs. I guess that whatever I talked to Amanda about in New Orleans must have given him the idea that what I was doing with the Corps might fit with that. I'm…"

"What do you mean?"

I slowed for the loop onto the beltway before replying, "We never really got into it. He was the host and couldn't talk. He said it wasn't anything immediate but that he'd be in touch."

"That's it?"

"That's it. But I could smell it, big bucks. Honest to God, Jen, he's apparently the owner, or the head of, or connected with, or represents – whatever - a lot of companies and deals with numbers that would impress even a federal budget officer."

"You've got more than six years of government service, Tommy, nice steady work. We're doing fine, just fine."

"Jen, come on; don't get so damned defensive; I'm going nowhere. Can't you see the difference between their world and ours? This under powered midget is no Lexus, and while I'll admit some of the touches in their place were a little heavy, we could use a few more square feet in Mclean or Langley."

"I sized you up against those big timers and you look as good as them any day. I don't care where they buy their suits; your Men's Warehouse outfit looked as good on you as anything in there."

I burst out laughing for the first time that evening, "That's sweet, but it's location that counts...and what kind of wheels deliver you there. Besides, like I said, we're as good as them any day, and I've been working on my abs," I said with a set grin. Man, I was still pursuing peace in the valley.

"You've got a really good job – with a future – and we've got a nice home and family. Don't you worry me, Tommy. I'm really uncomfortable with them. That pair is way too slick for us."

"Relax, Babe, I can handle myself. But my future with the Corps - if I stay there - is to move in lockstep with the guys I came in with. Most of 'em don't have any trouble with that, but I really want for us to have a future…for us, really."

"I already like the future I see. It was good enough for our folks and we're the same as them.

"God, your folks are happy as clams hunkered down in Springfield, and mine love it back in Pennsylvania. They feel like they're `in' in Happy Valley. We can have our own State College someday, too."

"Jen, I really want to be somebody. I didn't know when I signed on just how locked in I'd be from the first day, but I'll be pounding on that balky old calculator on that tin desk till I keel over on them."

I didn't mean to display my depression and inner angst, but I could tell that they were permeating the cockpit. "So please, Babe, just cool it for tonight, I don't want to talk about it anymore. O.K?"

I knew she wasn't finished with me but was letting it go without a response – for the moment.

SIX

"He called, Hon. Matt Roby wants me to meet him for lunch on Thursday at The Prime Rib," I was having a hard time containing my enthusiasm. It had been more than two weeks since the something less than magical night in McLean and I was beginning to think that my hopes and speculations never were or had been dashed, but he called - he did - even if it had slipped into the first week of June.

But the voice on the other end of the phone conversation was loaded with anxiety. "Lunch is fine but promise that you won't commit to anything until we talk about it," Jen implored.

"Where's The Prime Rib?"

'God, what a downer,' I thought. "Of course not; you know I wouldn't do that. But I'm going to take him up on the lunch. The Prime Rib's on K Street and it's the place where all the big deals go down – the real deals, but not mine." I clicked off abruptly but realized that hanging up in the second millennium isn't quite what it was in old black and white gangster noir movies when the phone hit the cradle with a bang and a bounce.

She never heard of The Prime Rib! No doubt, but then again, neither did I until the invite. I couldn't help but laugh at myself.

Thursday came and I was alive. Stepping out of the car at the garage at Pentagon City Mall, my nerves were on edge as I checked my necktie and was irritated again by the need for it. Ties! I couldn't believe there are restaurants that still `prefer' ties. And I really couldn't believe that Matt thought that's what it would take to impress me. Shit, I was ready to sit up, roll over and beg for a Big Mac.

After checking my parking location one last time, I walked through the garage to the entrance of the mall and passed the stores on my way down to the Metro station in the bowels of the building. Hell of design that mall, you can't get to the trains from the garage without passing half of the stores on at least one floor for your trouble.

After only a short wait during off peak service, I boarded a Blue Line Train and picked a seat near the transit system map posted adjacent to the car door. I wanted to make certain that I didn't wind up in Shady Grove or some other stop halfway to West Virginia. This was one lunch I wanted to make on time.

Living and working in Virginia, I was no longer as familiar with downtown DC as when I was a student at George Mason and went into Georgetown on many a Saturday night. I strained to decipher the muffled notice statements by the train operator at every stop after we left Arlington National Cemetery. It was like I was from Kansas and I've only lived here all my life. I thought, 'Hey, I'm not nervous! But why can't he get the damn marbles out his mouth for Christ's sake?' I was making an effort – unsuccessfully - to convince myself that it was the train operator who was screwed up rather than me. While the train was not nearly full, I shoved my way to be near the door as it slid open and only after I felt the platform at the Farragut

West station under my feet did my anxiety begin to recede to manageable levels.

Checking my watch for what seemed the hundredth time and finding that I was still more than ten minutes early I stepped to the right on the escalator and relaxed as those in a rush raced briskly past on my left. Realizing that I was going to be early, I detoured through the small park in the center of Farragut Square which had always been a pleasant place for an interlude at lunch time in fair weather. The girl watching was often first rate, especially since ground zero for female pulchritude in the District was within rock throwing distance from the spot.

After a brief swing through the park that confirmed my recollections about the eye candy, I reluctantly but resolutely walked through the great white cliffs of the marble canyon that is K Street to The Prime Rib and set the process in motion by announcing to the greeter that I was with Matt Roby. At the sound of the name, he snapped to attention like a soldier in a barrack when there's a surprise visit by a general officer.

"Mr. Roby is on his way, Mr. Phelan. He telephoned and asked me to tell you that he'll be here in just a few minutes. If you'll follow me, I'll take you to his table," the smile was pasted on and the mood was obsequious. At least Matt knew the protocol that the over dog was to show up after the anxious moron was given time to consider his lowly status.

`Hey, I'm just with him; relax,' was the message I tried to send telepathically, but the greeter moved as if he were guiding royalty.

"This is Mr. Roby's regular table," I was advised of the out of the way alcove that was very private. Turning to the tuxedoed young man who had somehow attached himself to our train, the greeter explained, "This is Charles; he'll be your server today, Mr. Phelan. If there's anything you need, just tell him and we'll do everything we can to make it happen."

"While you wait for Mr. Roby, sir, may I get you something to drink?"

'What's Matt's usual, Charles?"

"Mr. Roby often has a vodka martini, a la James Bond, sir – shaken, not stirred."

"I'll try one of those," I said with my own best smile pasted on as Charles backed away as if I were some kind of Maharajah. I couldn't help but be impressed by the stylized Kabuki moves. Damn, Roby's probably so used to this crap by now that he believes it. I knew the bastard was smart and ambitious and lucky when he aced me out on Swenson, but the house and this BS are way beyond my projections. What was it again that I had him slated for? Oh, yeah, bouncer in a strip joint. I couldn't help but smile at the ancient image.

After what I thought to be the perfect interlude, Charles came with my drink, and just as he set it before me, the host trailed by Matt Roby came floating into view.

"I see that they're treating you right, Tom. Way to go, guys," Matt said and added, "I'll have one of those, Charles."

"Right away, Mr. Roby," were the parting words as both employees scurried off wearing wide smiles.

I jumped to attention and Matt grasped my hand as if I were a long missing buddy returning from the Battle of the Bulge. "Sorry I'm late; business sometimes can't wait. Glad you could make it; I've been wanting to meet with you for some time."

'He has to have two inches on me, but somehow over ten years the asshole's shrunk three. Still no sign of a gut on Mr. Touchdown;

how the hell does he do that? Gut- check; hair – full no loss of color – check; shoulders – health club – check; overall – perfect – check. But he fires blanks – so I was told or thought I was told.'

We made small talk on the wonders of The Prime Rib until Charles arrived with Matt's drink. As the waiter retreated, Matt proposed a toast, "To a renewal of friendship and to prosperous days!"

I gave him my best smile and said, "I'll gladly drink to that." Renewal of friendship? I guess we all remember our high school days a little differently. Our quarterback must have taken too many shots to the head to remember that he barely recognized my existence in those days.

"Everything's delicious, don't even look at the numbers; the company can handle it," Roby said easily.

`You said it, pal,' I thought as I prepared to order the Maine Lobster Bisque for openers and then Filet Oscar. When I placed the order with Charles, I watched Matt carefully for any sign of flinching – not a one. 'Maybe he is for real.'

As we settled into our second martinis, Matt got down to business, "These are beginning to look like the worst of times – bad as they come, but as Rhett Butler educated Scarlet, that's often when the greatest opportunities present themselves. One of my companies has been invited to participate in the development of a major resort project in Mexico. The area north of Cancun is going to be developed into hotels and spas that will dwarf what's already there on the Yucatan.

"None of the really sharp people are spending now, and I guarantee you that the real estate bubble we're watching expand is going to burst with a vengeance that will make the dotcom fiasco look like a walk in the park. The people who advise me insist that the best thing to do right now is to accumulate cash and wait for the deleveraging that's bound to happen.

"That, my friend, is when we'll pounce with our cash; we'll leverage again like we're Archimedes reincarnated. No matter what they say it's leverage that makes our system hum. But cold hard cash will be king when we're ready to buy back in, and at that point we're going to need somebody to mind our interests on the project. I think you might be that person, Tom. If you've got the guts to join the team, it will be well worth your while."

"That's very flattering, Matt, but would that job be located here or Mexico?"

Roby smiled, "Oh, yeah...definitely. I should have been clearer; it's in contract management, kind of like what I expect you do with the Corps of Engineers. The job will be here in Arlington. It'll be quite some time in the future, and when it is a go, we'll install our own clerk of the works on site to make sure that the bricks and mortar stuff is up to snuff. We've got a good civil engineer on a job in Ecuador and we'll shift him over to Cancun if and when the Mexican government gives us the OK

"The contract manager will have to fly down maybe once every three or four months. Be assured it'll be good duty, but your job will definitely be out of our Arlington office.

"While the economy – ours and the worlds' – looks great to the fools looking at the real estate upslope, there'll be great opportunities for those with cash at the ready.

"I get reports from our rep on the ground that things are holding up well in Cancun. She's sharp as a tack but has conflicts of interest – she loves it there - and has no technical background."

I was wide awake at the scenario that Roby was laying out, and he kept boring in on my vulnerabilities, "The reason I wanted to get together with you is to see if you might be willing to take a couple of days off work to fly down to Cancun to get an impression of the resorts that are there today. You know: does it look like occupancy rates are somewhat close to what they say? Are the tourists dropping bundles in the casinos? Anything that strikes you. Naturally, we'll make it worth your time: a reasonable consulting fee plus expenses."

Matt finished his second martini and waived off Charles who sprinted in to check the need for a refill. "We're talking many millions, by far the biggest commitment our consortium has ever made. This would move our company close to the top of big time international gaming and resorts, so I need an outsider to make an informal appraisal and give it to me straight. This isn't a job offer, but I think that you might have a better appreciation of what we're up to and whether you might consider becoming part of the operation down the road.

"What do you think?"

Playing for time, I slowly examined my drink and took a swallow. "Yeah, I could do that. When would you want me to go?" while trying to strike a professional pose of semi-detached interest in the proposal. All the while I was thinking, 'Good Lord, I can't believe I said that without jumping up and down.'

"Maybe over a weekend – say Friday to Monday – as soon as you can do it…maybe in a couple of weeks… if your schedule works."

"I'll see if I can get the time off and give you a call," I said while thinking, `Don't sweat it, buddy boy, I'll make it work.'

The rest of the lunch was a blur as I tried to pay attention to the small stuff that Roby had reverted to after dropping the proposal on me, and it wasn't until I awakened to full consciousness in the Pentagon City parking garage that I was able to shut off my surreal fantasy of how life might be if I were able to escape the wilds of Ft. Belvoir.

'Shit, Mama ain't gonna like this.' I turned over alternative explanations in my mind as I made my way south on Shirley Highway but had no final alibi even as I pulled into the carport. `Less than a minute to go; better polish one of those jewels or dig up a shiny new one,' I thought as I reached for the knob on the kitchen door.

Jen rushed to greet me with a peck on the lips. She smile broadly and said, "How'd it go?"

"I'm flying to Cancun, Mexico in two weeks to scout my future job," I said with great enthusiasm.

"But you said you wouldn't make any decisions till after we talked."

Fully expecting the blast, I soothed her anxieties, "Just kidding, hon; it's just a one-time trip, not a job commitment. In fact, it's a chance to see what working for him would be like without getting in too deep. It's…"

Her anger and fear were obvious, "Haven't you figured it yet. I don't trust those people. I didn't like them in high school and I don't want to get involved with them now. They're…"

"Jen, do you have even a clue how much I don't like my job? How dead end it looks to me? I'm not quitting, but this could be the chance of a lifetime. In the meantime, all he's asking is for me to fly down, look around and make a report on what I think of the place and the prospects for his company. I can do it in a couple of hours after getting back to…"

"How much is he going to pay you?"

"He didn't say… and I didn't ask, but…"

"But, but – you never even asked. God, Tommy, he could be taking you to the cleaners – a crappy flight, a hovel for a hotel and, `Oh, here's a hundred for your trouble.'"

"Look, Jen, I don't have any more time to talk, but if your scenario is the one that comes true, it'd be the best thing that ever happened. It'd be over. Got it?"

There was a long pause. "I still don't like it."

How about that! Out of comebacks for the first time in her life.

SEVEN

"**M**r. Phelan, you're booked in first class with full Sky High Club pass privileges on both legs of your trip to Cancun and, of course, on your return flights as well." I got the news, my ticket and an airline company packet as the proceedings became surreal; the employees were falling all over themselves to take care of me. Bowing, scraping and fawning were the order of the day. It was as if Mr. Thomas Phelan was very rich and powerful but at the same time extraordinarily fragile. I – `he' in the third person - was guided to the airline's private lounge where attendants saw to my -`his' - every need and whim – at least as they related to beverages and reading material. Hey, not bad!

As boarding time approached, I had to smile as a really bad ancient joke popped into my head: in the 1920s a rich college age Boston Brahmin kid was being carried from one of those big Back Bay brownstone mansions on Commonwealth Avenue to the family roadster by a pair of muscular Irishmen when a horrified neighbor approached the socialite mother with, "Dorothea, my dear, I'm so sorry, but can't your poor Everett walk?"

"Of course he can walk, Martha, but thank heaven he doesn't have to."

When my flight was announced, I smiled and looked around just to be certain that I wasn't going to be borne aboard the plane by a phalanx of uniformed litter bearers. Instead, they just hustled me conspicuously to the front of the line and gently escorted me to my oversize seat even before they dealt with the lame, aged and the little darlings strapped into strollers. I was then treated to the embarrassing stares of hoi polloi enviously sniveling as they passed me on their way to their little people's seats in the back of the bus. As the boarding progressed, a wan smile rose and fell as I remembered John Barrow's description of French peasants passing through Versailles and being afforded the privilege of watching the king dine. I almost exclaimed, 'Excuse me, steward, but do you have sufficient escargot onboard?'

Aside from being treated as much like royalty as an airline is able: wine, a gourmet meal – in the Irish sense of the term - and all of the boiling face cloths one could hope for in the course of a lifetime of gobbling down greasy fast food, I was given the chance to observe the behavior of my six obviously far more experienced first class cabin mates and made a mental note that if this were ever again part of my life experience I would assume their regal behavior of complete indifference to the process and the human flotsam with which I had to share oxygen.

As the histrionics continued throughout the first leg of the flight, I wasn't a bit surprised by my joyous welcome in Miami and then again in Cancun.

It was already well after two in the afternoon local time when we touched down on the tarmac on the Yucatan. Despite having only one small suitcase, clearing Mexican customs turned out to be an hour long ordeal. Entering the terminal I saw nothing but a gauntlet of hawkers that I was going to have to run if I were ever to reach my resort. "No, I don't want a timeshare!

"Stick that pyramid, Pal!

"No, no, a thousand times no!"

Man, were they ever persistent, but I finally spotted a very attractive young woman at the front of another line of greeters holding a small sign of welcome for, `Sr. Thomas Phelan'. I wondered if Matt Roby knew or dealt with any ordinary looking women. It must be hell to have to deal only with nines and tens, and I wondered if this could possibly rub off on his middle management team as I straightened my posture and sucked in my gut and sauntered to join Juanita Perez, my guide for the weekend according to the information in Matt's company packet.

Her smile was so genuine that I was already beaming as we met. "Senorita Perez, I presume?"

"Si, Sr. Phelan. Welcome to Cancun."

"Mucho Gracias…well that about does it for me en Espanol. Please call me Tom."

The smile never faltered as she replied in virtually unaccented English, "Tom it is; I'm Juanita."

We strode outside the terminal into the brilliant sunshine of the Yucatan. The pain from the direct rays and the resulting heat was intense and immediate, and I thought for a second that I'd taken the door to a crematorium.

Seeing my discomfort, Juanita brought me back to the moment with, "My car is right over there, just a very short walk," she said while pointing toward what was obviously the high rent district for private vehicles. The trunk of the Mercedes convertible rose as if in a salute of welcome for me as we approached.

"Nice wheels."

"We have a first class company, Tom, and we demonstrate it in many ways."

Juanita pulled out onto the main road to the resort and the powerful air conditioner quickly lowered the temperature to a level sufficient for me to begin breathing normally.

"I know how uncomfortable you must be. The shock of the sun and the heat when you leave the terminal is almost unbearable, but you'll be fine once we get settled at the resort. That the sun can fry eggs on almost any surface here is difficult for people from the States and Canada to comprehend, but you really will be able to cope, trust me."

We drove for miles through what had to be the world's longest allee of mangrove trees, but soon on the horizon the string of resorts loomed like what I first thought was a series of updated Mayan temples but which turned out to be more accurately a strip of hotels like those of Miami Beach. As we approached our destination, the Casa Magna resort, she smiled and said, "You're preregistered, so expect to have to sign in only as a formality. Everything is covered, so don't hesitate to ask for whatever you desire."

'Whatever you desire, Tommy boy,' whoa, that could cover a multitude of sins I thought but said, "You're extremely well organized."

"Matt Roby runs a tight ship. Our clients, customers and friends count on us, and we do our best to deliver," she said turning to me with a quick smile as she pulled up at the valet pick-up station.

"I'll be with you during registration and wait in the lobby while you settle in. I assure you that this is one of the finest resorts in Cancun, but if there is anything that isn't just right or that doesn't meet your expectations, let me know, and I'll do everything possible to have it corrected. Understood?"

She seemed to hesitate, "Tom, this is a world class resort, a prideful place of pleasure and happiness. I hope that you've packed something a little less formal than this suit," she said as she lightly touched my lapel. "I know that you're here on business, but I assure you that you will be far more successful if you approach your work looking at least a little bit more like the other guests."

I couldn't help but laugh at the well rumpled buttoned down summer cement suit, my government uniform. "You may be onto something. I've got a couple of Hawaiian shirts that might look a little more touristy than this cheap version of a Washington power suit; I'll change as soon as I can."

Half an hour later as I stepped from the elevator into her line of sight in the lobby, I couldn't control my guffaw at the comical expression on Juanita's face. "I hope that you're not laughing at me. This wasn't easy to achieve," I said while sliding my hands over the front of my new outfit.

Exaggerating, I looked down at my blue palm tree festooned solar yellow Honolulu special draped over badly wrinkled tan cargo shorts and then beyond to my black sandals that framed my blindingly white feet and ankles that eased to an almost human hue at a vague tan line well below the knees, the product of two rounds of golf and a half a dozen fruitless visits to the Burke Lake Park driving range. Seeking eye contact with her, I asked, "What?" with a mock look of innocent confusion on my face.

"Perfect," she said with no effort to muffle her glee.

We sat on a sofa in the lobby, and I said, "Matt told me try to gauge how crowded the place felt and whether the people looked like they were having fun; simple subjective questions, eh?"

The idea that such a gorgeous creature might be with me in Cancun was beyond my wildest fantasies, but there she was sitting beside me looking like a dream, even if she was really just my baby sitter and not my companion. Her hair was pure anthracite, the deepest black imaginable but with highlights popping like brilliant diamonds at every turn of her head. The contrast with her peaches and cream complexion was startling and spectacular. Appearances are more important than reality – at least among the Phelan clan.

'Wait till Jimmy Frawley hears about this,' I thought, and of course he would, with no embellishment whatsoever, naturally.

"Are you from around here?" I asked, attempting to break the ice.

"No. I'm from Mexico City originally. I came here with another of Matt Roby's companies about three years ago…after four years at UCLA polishing my English. Does it show?"

"It sure does. You have hardly the trace of an accent, just an occasional over-trill of the `r's – which by the way is very attractive."

She smiled and lowered her eyes for a fraction of a second, but beyond that ignored the crack. "Have you been to Mexico before?"

"Never, but I've been looking forward to visiting Cancun for years."

The bantering continued as I did my damndest to flirt with her while at the same time trying to gauge the guests' happiness quotients as they promenaded about the lobby and out to the beach. After about ten minutes, it became clear that both efforts were losers. "I'm already tired of sitting. Why don't we stroll by the pool or go out onto the beach or something? Anything but squatting here; I have to get off my duff and look around."

"Just give me a minute to freshen up," she said and walked away.

When she returned, I asked, "Could I have heard right? Two young women walked past me and I overheard heard them saying that they were going skinny dipping?"

"But of course. It's a little known feature in Cancun that those with a little spunk about them have every chance to indulge their daring by exposing as much of themselves to the sun and to each...Oh, well."

"Why don't we take a little dip?" I said with a grin.

"Why Mr. Phelan, I hardly know you," she said demurely.

"But you said that I should ask for whatever I desired."

"Did I? I couldn't have said that...or meant anything like skinny dipping. Could I? And I certainly don't remember saying that your every desire would come true."

We continued to flirt, but the need to prepare a report began to invade my thoughts. On the job for fifteen minutes and already it's obvious; this isn't going to be as easy as I'd thought. 'What the hell is it I'm supposed to gauge again?'

Whatever, we began to meander through the resort. I still couldn't believe that such a beautiful, well turned out woman would be caught dead in the company of an ordinary government slob like me, and I was mildly uncomfortable at the idea that everyone was watching us instead of the way we had it programmed. "Aside from the fact that every guy in the joint is ogling you whenever they get the chance, everything I see just seems to match what I think should be normal – given that I don't know what I'm talking about. Got any idea what Roby wants from me?"

"A couple of hours on the ground and you've reached pretty much the same conclusion as I did over the course of several years. For many months I've been trying to tell Matt that everything is great down here. Maybe he just wants you to confirm it. To me, if things are this good during terrible times, the project to the north of here looks to me like it would be a winner. Did he mention the political problems with the project?"

I was caught short, "Not a word. What's up?"

"Environmental groups in the States are upset at the prospect of such a huge development. As far as they're concerned it's just another disastrous mega project. You know how it is; developers don't care about unspoiled beaches, coral reefs, sea turtles, birds, the whole nine yards...and more. They're making all kinds of trouble for the politicians in Mexico City, and they're agitating with their gringo counterparts to involve Washington."

"Roby knows about this?"

"He can't help but be aware of it if he reads my reports and keeps up with the news. Actually, I'm pretty sure that he's up to speed, but given the economic situation, I suppose it's not that big a worry at this point in the project. Besides, I know that lobbyists for the consortium are at work in Mexico City and Washington."

"Maybe I could add a little to your stuff. Any chance we could have a look around up there?"

"I thought that would be the best way to do it, so I just happened to rent a dune buggy for Sunday. It's gorgeous country and we'll have great time."

The way she looked made it hard for me to keep my mind on business, and it was getting worse by the minute. "How do I get a drink?"

"Just walk over to the bar - like that one," she said pointing to a full service bar that was situated on the edge of a beautiful swimming pool just outside the lobby and in sight of the Gulf;

actually the bar was incorporated into the design of the pool itself. "They're everywhere in the resort - and order up. Just say the word and up they pop," she said while pointing to the bar nearest them. "I could use one myself. Let's go."

After picking up our margaritas we walked casually to a pair of unoccupied chairs and slid under the shade of the umbrella. "These beach chairs are perfect for people watching, but I'm not sure that Roby will get his money's worth by the way this is beginning," I said.

"You'll have to be a quick study on the Cancun lexicon, Tom. These are `lounge chairs', and not to worry, I have no doubt that your trip report will be outstanding."

Still, I couldn't keep my mind focused on my task. `My God, she's smashing,' I thought. Every move she made was elegant as the taut muscles under her vibrant flesh rippled like the waves in the pool. I was helpless to stop my peripheral vision from being drawn ever more toward her and away from the patrons I was supposed to be watching who were fast disappearing from my radar screen.

I kept fighting the urge to focus my attention on Juanita overtly and continued to pose half hearted questions about the resort and the next project. I thought, `Damn, she hangs on my words like she cares. What the hell am I supposed to do? She has got to be the most gorgeous creature I've ever flirted with; I better have another belt.'

Almost on command, a young waiter approached and asked if we'd like refills. "I know I would; make it a double tequila.

How about you, Juanita?"

"I'll have another one of those – but regular size," she said with enthusiasm.

It became surreal; I was alone with one of the most attractive women in Cancun and by the minute the alcohol was kicking the hell out of the little man in my head.

About an hour later, I heard and felt my stomach growl. "I'm starving; how about dinner?"

"I thought you'd never ask. We can stay here and grab something light, or we can go to one of the several restaurants inside the resort. May I suggest La Capilla Argentina Steakhouse? It's one of my very favorites among all of the wonderful restaurants in all of Cancun. The steaks are directly from the pampas and broiled to absolute perfection.

"It's covered either way... for all guests," she added, "The business model is really well thought out, and everyone has a great time."

"Should I change my outfit?"

"I don't know what you mean; you're formal now, but if we opt for dinner, you should shape up a little – open shirt, a summer jacket, trousers...anything to instill a little romance and decorum; not that you aren't dressed for success right now. " she said with a smirk.

After finishing a wonderful dinner at La Capilla Argentina which included the local catch of the day and the tastiest rib eye I'd ever eaten and, of course, two more margaritas, I pleaded for a time out, "It's almost nine and I'm completely wiped out. I need a shower, and I hate to admit it but a half hour nap would clear my brain – at least a little.

"Would you mind terribly?" The pleading in my voice was genuine, too damn genuine, but in the state I was in, I no longer cared.

"You've been on the go all day, so it's no wonder that you're exhausted. Let's go to our rooms and freshen up. Maybe we'll feel like taking advantage of the night life after a recess. I..."

I was startled into the moment and cut her off with an incredulous, "You're staying here too?"

"I thought you knew. Your schedule is very tight, and…"

"Yeah, maybe you told me – Roby…or somebody; I don't know. Whatever, I absolutely have to turn in…at least for a bit."

I questioned whether I ever knew that she was booked into the resort and was damned if I could remember, but had I known, I sure as hell wouldn't have had so damn much to drink.

Although my gait was unaffected – at least I thought it was, she took my hand and steered me to the elevator. We were alone inside the car, and she asked, "Where's your key?"

As we walked to my room, I fumbled through all of my pockets before finding my wallet in the same hip pocket in which I always kept it since becoming an adult. "Now that's a surprise," I declared.

The plastic key card was exposed and Juanita took it and quickly opened the door and guided me in. "Everything looks fine, but if you find anything amiss just knock," she said pointing at the door between the rooms.

"You're kidding me?" I said, truly stunned.

She smiled broadly and replied, "Would I do that? Now, if you're set, I'm going to my room."

By this time I was very wide awake but exhausted and really smashed. "Yeah, I'm set. You're right next door? Right there?" I said while pointing at the interior door.

"That's right, right in there, but it's locked from the other side, so I'm leaving the way I came in…And don't knock unless there's an emergency. Now, get some sleep. Good night, Tom."

Still not thinking as clearly, as she walked away, I added my own very confused, "Good night."

EIGHT

The digital clock on the table next to my bed indicated that it was two-ten, the middle of the damn night. I was wide awake but thoroughly confused as I used to occasionally find myself when I was young and single after drinking too much and attempting to sleep it off. It took what seemed like forever to place myself in my room at the resort in Cancun.

How the hell long had I been out cold? What day was it? Only after six minutes had silently passed did clarity begin to form in my mind. "Whoa; how many margaritas does it take to knock a stupid Irishman on his ass? About half as many as I had," I said under my breath.

My head throbbed like a bass drum marking time for a marching band. `How can I hear what isn't making any noise?' I sat up and dropped my feet to the floor. "Well at least it doesn't hurt… too much," I whispered…not nearly as bad as I regularly endured on the Saturday night after final exams.

Decisively, I fell back into the bed determined to snooze till breakfast, normal breakfast time, but it took only a couple of tosses and turns for me to realize that there would be no more sleep this night. Eyes wide open, I found myself staring at the blank ceiling until the clock showed two thirty-nine. As often happened on

dark endless nights when I was a kid, my latent triskaidekapho-
bia made an unwanted appearance and it mattered not whether
it was the number thirteen itself or any multiple of it that I could
easily compute, I could not allow myself to get out of bed until a
luckier set of digits appeared on fear of...what? At two-forty-two,
I made my move.

In the bathroom, I splashed cold water on my face and
attempted an inventory: `clean but unshaven; not too bad.' After
the inspection, I combed my hair, put on the resort supplied ter-
rycloth robe over my navy blue pajama shorts, checked myself
out in the full length mirror and whispered, "Adequate. You, my
man, are in dire need of a sleeping pill, so let's give it a go."

Walking resolutely to the double door separating my room
from Juanita's, I unlatched my side, pulled open the door and
knocked softly on her door. After about thirty seconds without a
response, I rapped again, this time quite a bit louder.

As I was about to knock again, I heard a faint female voice, "Is
that you, Tom?"

"Yes."

"It's the middle of the night," she said, pointing out the obvious.

"I can't sleep, and you said I could knock if there was an emergency," I said in the most plaintive tone I could muster.

The latch clicked and the door opened to a room in which
every light was blazing.

I squinted but was able to note that she was also wearing one
of the snow white resort robes. Hair tousled and eyes puffy, I
thought she was gorgeous. "I've been awake for hours," I fibbed
as my heart pounded.

"Come in - but for the record, I was sound asleep," she said
with more than a hint of annoyance in her voice.

"I'm really sorry. I thought that you might be having trouble sleeping too. It really seemed to qualify as a calamity."

I saw that she was becoming more alert by the second and judged from her slight but rising smile that her first reaction might no longer be the operable paradigm. I reached my arm about her waist very casually, placed my hand gently but firmly on the small of her back and applied very light pressure. Shockingly, it was more than enough and she flew toward me as the robe slipped magically to the floor revealing nothing but firm flesh that was clearly mine for the taking.

Embracing and kissing passionately, we tangoed toward the bed. Shedding my robe, my eyes filled with wonder at the gorgeous body that was responding to my every move and touch. Seduction was never my strong suit, so it was more of an out of body experience as everything went my way with this gorgeous creature.

Given my level of expertise and obvious eagerness, in minutes she said with a sly smile, "If this was an old movie, it would be time for a cigarette."

"If this was a movie, we'd be fading to black. How about cutting the lights?"

"That wasn't so important a few minutes ago," she said, chuckling.

Reaching for my robe that was spread on the floor beside her, she pulled it on and moved from lamp to lamp returning the night. Returning to the bed, she pressed the button on the lamp on the nightstand nearest her. "I doubt that you'll have trouble sleeping now," she added with mock seriousness.

"Sleep? Sleep? Who wants to sleep?" I said reaching to gather her once again.

NINE

I awakened at first light, completely spent, and became aware that a set of minor problems were raising their ugly heads: guilt and shame. My little man - silent as I performed previously unknown feats of graceful romantic gymnastics - was in full throat about my degradation. With the speed of light, I gathered my shorts and robe and fled the scene. Closing my door quickly but nearly silently, I twisted the latch with my last remaining resource of strength and checked to be sure that it was secure. `Shame, Tommy Phelan! You've been a bad, bad boy.' Racing for the shower, I scrubbed mightily to exorcise the demons my conscience was parading before me, but it was a losing effort. Toweling off, I realized that if I didn't ease up blood would soon be oozing from innocent pores due to the scraping that a soft terry cloth can manage when wielded like a hair shirt. "Hey, straighten up; no harm, no foul. It was just a one night stand, so lighten up," I whispered to my little guy, "What happens in Cancun stays in Cancun; right?

"Yes, I confirmed eagerly," at a much higher decibel level.

Flopping on the bed, I fully expected the torture to go on, but surprisingly I drifted off quickly and was comatose until awakened by the incessant ringing of the phone.

"Good morning, man who could not sleep. Did I wake you?" Juanita asked.

"From the dead," I said while searching for the time. "God, it's almost nine; we've got to get going. Good thing you called or I'd have slept till my plane took off on Monday."

She laughed and said, "Well you did complain that you couldn't sleep."

"Give me ten minutes and I'll meet you in the restaurant."

Arriving in the restraunt ahead of her and before I could think about my needs, a steaming decanter of freshly brewed coffee arrived. Pouring a cup, I looked up to see her floating toward me and greeted her with, "You look really great. Are you ready for a day of resort hopping?"

Her smile was even more radiant than when she greeted me at the airport. "I'm looking forward to it.

"I think you'll find that the atmosphere in most of the resorts is comparable; the differences being price and amenities. The vacation packages are all great bargains, whatever their level; the differences really turn out to be mostly in the elegance of the hotel and the number of wait and support staff. It's all first-rate, and that's why I'm convinced that the area north of here will be just as big a winner and why I keep sending positive messages to Matt. "

I smiled and said, "Hey, you're lobbying me again and you know that you're not supposed to be doing that. Matt says that I have to make an independent appraisal of the situation. I gather that he knows your take on the project very well and wouldn't want you filling my innocent head with your wild ideas."

She laughed. "You think I like living in this hole populated by beautiful young Americans, Brits, Canadians and Germans and all the while enjoying virtually unlimited access to world class resorts? That I might want this to go on indefinitely? Surely you jest, Sr. Phelan."

"Maybe, but I've never been treated better by someone with a conflict of interest." I was happy that she was making such an easy switch of gears. My conscience was still making rumbles and I wanted to get on with the job in order to confuse and confound my ethics leprechaun still further.

We chose the buffet and hurried through breakfast to begin the workday. After freshening up in our rooms, we met in the lobby and made the trek to her car which was parked far away from the cares of everyday life, like all other reminders of home and work.

The hours flew by as we scrambled from one resort hotel to the next and early in the tour I became convinced of the correctness of Juanita's assessment of the state of the hospitality business in Cancun. The only thing that remained was to take a look at the land under option and guess what it might look like fully developed and populated by even more young lovers, tourists and high rollers.

As the day progressed, I was consciously holding down my craving for rich food and most especially the margaritas, wanting desperately to arrive back in Fairfax in a state of health and well being not too different from that in which I'd departed. It was still early Saturday, and my queasy stomach and throbbing temples encouraged me to dial down the extracurricular activities if I were ever to meet that goal and make it home without a wheelchair.

"Tell you what; let's go back to our place for lunch and I'll write up the first half of my report before dinner."

I didn't mention the other elements of my proposed activity, but judging from her warm smile and ready agreement, I had the feeling that her schedule might be flexible.

Awakening an hour and a half into the proposed fifteen minute catnap, I found that Juanita was missing from my room. I showered, without nearly as much guilt as before, and began working on the report. It flowed easily. `Of course it's easy; there's no data. Any moron could do this; it writes itself, especially since I've been getting line by line and paragraph by paragraph recitation from the resident expert.'

Nearing the end of the first half of the report, I heard a light knock on the door. "One second!" I saved the work, closed the laptop and rose to open the door.

She strode in smiling. "Thank goodness you're alright. I tried to rouse you a couple of times but there was no answer. If you hadn't responded this time I was going to call the house doctor – who happens also to be the local coroner. I thought perhaps that you had…"

"Died!" I cut her off and laughed.

"Maybe had a mild heart attack."

We embraced and kissed gently.

"I've got a pretty good start on my draft. How about we have something light for dinner and take in a show? I'm too pooped to do anything active, so…"

She cut me off with, "I was going to suggest just that. It sounds like a plan, but don't think you have to take me out; we could just stay in our rooms and read."

I laughed, "I'm not an invalid – yet – and there's a chance I can get through the evening without intravenous."

"Well I don't want to be held liable for any collapses that happen on my watch."

"Not to worry; my Blue Cross/Blue Shield covers ruptures of the heart."

"That wasn't the rupture I was concerned about," she said and laughed aloud.

"Enough, gentle-lady; go to your room and get ready for dinner and entertainment. Phase one of our job is complete."

Damned if we didn't stick to the plan.

When the evening ended, she said, "Thanks for a very nice time; I'm going to turn in. Should I keep a sharp ear for a knock in the night?"

"Definitely, but don't open without checking for an I.D. as I may be unconscious and unable to defend your honor," I said while reaching to embrace her.

TEN

Near the summer solstice, the sun was brilliant and white hot as it beat virtually straight down on our dune buggy as we drove north on the road from Cancun. Juanita was at the wheel and all the while continued to serve as the head of the chamber of commerce for the proposed development. The road quickly narrowed to two lanes and the quality of the pavement followed suit as the distance from the resorts increased. Her chatter on the great opportunities afforded by proposed development continued, but I paid little attention as I was wowed by the beauty of the seaside drive. The breeze from the road made the heat bearable, barely.

I finally interrupted her monologue with, "Tell you what: Why don't you just park this buggy under a palm tree somewhere along the way and let me nod off to get ready for my re-entry into the real world while you write my report for me. I completely agree with your analysis, and while you're at the top of your sales pitch, I'm half dead. Really, there's no need to drive on."

She laughed and said, "I'm sorry, but I'm so enthused about the project that I can't help myself. But I'll stop talking right now," she said with an exaggerated zipping motion for her lips.

"Not permanently, I hope."

She turned to me and zipped her smile again.

Continuing with only pleasant irrelevant banter for perhaps another thirty minutes, she suddenly pulled off the road and headed for a copse of about a dozen palm trees that were shading what appeared to be an abandoned and decrepit beach hut sporting mostly broken windows. Parking in the shade of the tallest tree, she turned to me and announced, "I'm not allowed to lobby, but nobody said anything about swimming being prohibited."

Hopping out of the buggy, she turned and pranced toward the Gulf shedding articles of apparel at almost every step. Racing into the Gulf that lay shimmering before her without any sign of waves or swells beyond those she was stirring with exaggerated kicks, I was rendered mute.

Advancing into the perfectly clear water up to her knees, she suddenly spun about and faced me. Cupping her hands into the shape of a megaphone, she shouted, "I know you now. You did say you wanted to skinny dip, right, Sr. Phelan?

"Well, aren't you coming?"

Kicking off my sandals, I leaped into the soft white sand and made a show of covering her every item with one of my own until my clothing supply was exhausted. Hopping over the last twenty yards of burning but exquisitely fine almost pure white sand, I joined her in the sparkling clear Gulf.

Embracing her, I said, "I saw this scene in *From Here to Eternity* but never dreamed that I'd live it."

"It's paradise isn't it?"

"I wouldn't know but it'll do until something better comes along."

We walked back to the dune buggy hand in hand bending along the route to recover our clothes but making no effort in any way to cover ourselves. Finding myself an innocent South Sea Islander in the nineteenth century, I turned unashamed to gaze on her glorious naturalness.

Juanita opened the satchel she had tossed into the back seat and pulled out a beach blanket, shook it open and placed it on the cool sand in the shade of the great palm.

"Bingo!"

"What?" she exclaimed.

"Just an old Ocean City, Maryland war whoop; you're making me feel eighteen again, but don't even think about it. It was just a kid's joke."

"For someone complaining that he was dying, you're doing a fantastic imitation of Lazarus."

"The opera always ends with the death of the hero. Besides, when I got off the plane my first thought was that you were a knockout, but the true meaning of the term never entered my mind until this very minute."

At that she guffawed. "Wow! Lame!"

ELEVEN

A s I pulled into the driveway, I ran a quick check of my systems: 'Rest – adequate, slept virtually all the way from Mexico to Washington - barely waking for the stop in Miami; appearance – thought to be OK, scrubbed well prior to leaving resort room; attitude: return of the hero, report done, set to resume life; all check.'

On stepping out of the Malibu and pushing the button to the trunk, I slammed the driver's door to alert the home front of my arrival and moved to retrieve my luggage.

The carport door to the kitchen swung open and Jen, very pregnant and carrying Ashley on her right hip pointed and said in a very excited voice, "Daddy's home! Daddy's home!"

Exchanging a quick peck on the lips, Jen said, "Thank God you're home; another day and I would have died. Ash was great, but Jackie…don't ask."

The little girl's round face burst into a sunny smile and she reached for me and interrupted the happy home coming, "Daddy home!"

Swinging her around, I said, "You bet I'm home, Sweetie… to stay."

I handed Ashley back to Jen and thought, 'God, with that house dress and swollen belly and a kid on her hip she looks like something straight out of the Great Depression. We gotta do better.'

"How was Cancun?" she said, appearing to force a tight smile.

"Amazing! Of course I didn't have time for anything but work. Had to hit all of the hotels and resorts on the Yucatan so playing was out of the question, but it looked like everyone was having lots of fun. Someday we'll have to do it. I'm sure you'd like it."

The smile faded. "It'll be a while."

'Jesus, what a freakin' downer,' I thought. 'I can't change anything and we're doing great, but she comes out to greet me like something out of American Gothic. What shit!'

"I brought you something, sweetie," I said smiling at Ashley. As soon as we got inside the kitchen I made a great show of opening my bag and pulling out the wrapped package. "For you, Sweetie."

Jen and Ashley tore at the paper and out popped a native costumed Mexican doll baby.

"Baby," Jen said.

That new appellation was repeated a dozen times before Ashley toddled off.

Jen sounded apprehensive, "Think anything will come of the trip?"

"Nothing but a check," I said with the broadest smile I could muster. "The project, if it ever happens, will be years away. In the meantime it's shuffle on down to Belvoir five days a week."

"Good!" she said with great emphasis.

Her negativity was really getting annoying, and I thought, 'I don't get it; we're living on the margin, but when a window is barely cracked open, she slams it shut before even a whiff of hope can get it. Is the damn glass half full or half empty? Let me know someday, will ya.' All the while I was doing my best performance of a guy jumping for joy at being home with his loved ones. I mean, it is home and they are the ones I truly care about but she wasn't making my reentry any easier; of course if I had just spent a long weekend in this zoo maybe I wouldn't be jumping for joy either. Whatever, we were both half frosted.

"I have to finish and package the report on the trip and drop it by the post office in the morning. I know you've been straight out here, but if you could keep Ash out of my hair for just a little while longer, I'd appreciate it," I said, trying to sound as pleasant as possible.

`And see if you can find that smile you lost a couple of years back while you're at it,' but as soon as the thought took shape, guilt set in big time. I'm raising hell – I mean hell - in Mexico with a great chic and she's working her buns off here in suburbia.

"Jen, remember that table book of New Yorker cartoons we had in the old place? I'm sorry for leaving you here smothered under by kids while I was practically lounging in one of the world's great playgrounds. One of my favorite cartoons in the book was of a woman with her kids clinging and crawling all over her, hair hanging, doing ironing with an open window on a sweltering day, and her old man says, 'I don't understand, Helen, you used to be such a fun person.' You're really wonderful. I love you and appreciate all that you do."

On Wednesday, my second day back at work, I was immersed in a contract file and was thoroughly startled when my phone rang, "Tom Phelan," I said, giving the usual governmentese for hello.

"Hi, it's me," was Jen's usual opening, but she was disciplined enough not to call me at work unless there was at least a semi-valid need to talk with me.

"What's up?"

"You got a letter from Matt Roby."

"Yeah? And."

"I opened it, and there's a three thousand dollar check in it."

"What?"

"You heard me. And there was a nice note saying that you're report was brilliant, just what he needed. And, and he said he was sorry that he hadn't worked out your fee beforehand and was hoping that $750.00 a day was satisfactory."

I was out of my skin with excitement, "I told you they could help us, Jen. There's gold in them thar hills. Man, seven hundred and fifty a day; how about them apples, Babe?"

"I'm proud of you, Tommy. This will really help; you know how we've fallen behind with Sean and all.

"Hurry home. I'm going to run to Giant to get us a steak, and I'm going to ask your Mom if I can drop off Ash and Jackie for the night – so we can celebrate."

"That, Love, sounds like a plan," I said, all the while thinking, `Damn it, I told you. Why don't you listen to me?' Then I added, "Stick with me, Babe; we're going places."

TWELVE

The boss's office door was open and I knocked as I stepped in and greeted him.

"I haven't seen you since you got back. So how was the vacation?" John Barrow asked, smiling.

I had given him a very limited heads up on what was happening before I left. Naturally, there was little need to give him all the details on Roby and my plans for when I left the Corps of Engineers. "It was a great place, but I was too busy on a personal project to really get down and dirty," I replied, trying to cut off the discussion. "What's up? Your voice mail said that you wanted to see me."

Pointing to a chair, he said, "We're making some changes around here and they involve you. The division's budget is being cut, and we're eliminating your branch. Callahan's job is disappearing with it and we're breaking up his staff and shifting everybody around. I've been running the division and doing Fred's job and it's starting to show – and not in the best ways."

He spoke more quietly, "I've been impressed with your work, Tom, and I want to keep you in my office as my special assistant and to have you manage the Native American and Alaska Native accounts that Fred handled himself. Since they're an entirely different species from our usual contract bill of fare, I think we'd do well to keep them centralized at the division level.

"Fred and I had talked about you quite a few times before he was killed and we agreed that you were a cut above the other young contracting officers. Your accounting skills are way beyond what we ordinarily see and we agreed that you had a great future with the Corps. But along came the tragedy and none of that thinking is still relevant. So it's on to plan B which may be even better for you."

"Thanks, I appreciate the compliment."

"It's well deserved. If you agree to the proposal, we'll start the transition on an acting basis and get it done officially as quickly as possible. Given a couple of months, I'm pretty sure that we can swing a promotion for you. We'll set you up next door to me in Fred's old office.

"Well, what do you think?"

"I appreciate you thinking of me, John; that sounds great and you can count on me to do my best."

"Done. I'll have a list of all your present contracts drawn up to show you which branches you should deliver them to. When that's done, you can move your stuff in next door and I'll give you all of the Alaska files," John said as he rose and extended his hand. "Welcome aboard; you deserve it."

The next Thursday morning, Barrow stuck his head into my new office. "So how's it going in the new digs?"

Startled by the interruption, I looked up. "Whew! I was so into this file I didn't see you. I may be crazy, John, but I've got problems with this Alaska contract – real problems. It looks to me like we've got a huge turd on the table. I'll keep digging but this looks like we may have a case of fraud. If I'm right, this is no nickel and dime cookie jar pilfering but maybe an inside job in the millions. It will…"

Barrow coughed and after the spasm subsided, he barked his way through with, "Well keep on it and brief me as soon as you can. We can't let anything that's even the slightest bit suspicious get by," and backed out and walked into his office.

I pondered the situation before returning to the file and thought, 'I don't get it. This is so friggin' obvious but both he and Callahan signed off. I've run these numbers ten times if I've run 'em once, and they always come out the same way: we're being ripped off big time. And this damn daisy chain of companies – phony bastards if I ever saw any - is so friggin' long it'll take me a month to figure out where the dough's going.'

I skipped lunch and ran the numbers still again, but true to the pattern, they again came up tilt. I watched for Barrow to return to his office and grabbed my files and marched in on him.

"Close the door," he ordered.

As I returned to the chair in front of his desk, he said, "What've you got?"

"More than enough phony numbers to scare the crap out of me. If I'm right, John, you've signed off on some awful contracts and invoices that might put your butt in a sling. I'd say the same about Fred, but he doesn't have to answer for his actions any more.

"It looks like we've overpaid on this huge data processing contract by maybe a third and that alone could be as much as five…maybe even six million bucks. I've gone over the numbers again and again, and they stink to high heaven. I took a quick look at a couple of other of these contracts, and they all look rotten. Tell me I'm wrong; there has to be an answer."

Before he could begin to explain, I went on, "Then there's a daisy chain of companies that I'll have to sort through, and until I get that done, I won't be able to tell you where the money went."

As I waited for Barrow to gather his thoughts, I suddenly stumbled on what had to be the answer in the recesses of my brain that solved the puzzle and absolved everyone. The epiphany was obvious. `Of course, this is one of those black budget items, the kind they use to fund top secret shit for the CIA and other intelligence outfits. That has to be it.' In that instant I relaxed and waited for Barrow to reassure me.

John suddenly stopped his hacking and focused his gaze directly on my eyes, "You're going to have to hear me out on this, Tom. This is a very complex business."

I was already feeling better as my analysis made more sense every second I waited for Barrow's confirmation.

"The bottom line, Tom, is that you've stumbled onto a fraudulent racket. Fred Callahan got caught up in this and sold his office, and it wasn't long before I got bullied and blackmailed into the scheme."

I was horrified but was unable to say anything before he continued.

"It breaks my heart to admit that I'm corrupt. I've sold my office. I'm ashamed but I couldn't help myself; they had me over a barrel.

"We – I'll get to that in a minute – have been at this for a couple of years and you're right it's in the millions, probably over fifteen million so far with maybe double that in the pipeline."

Barrow was talking quickly and softly and at this point looking down at his hands that were joined as if in prayer, "With Fred dead, the company…the outfit…the organization…whatever you want to call it, needed another partner, and we – really `they' - settled on you. So, it's you join and we all get richer than Midas, or you walk out of here, and the rest of us go to jail for years. You've…"

I couldn't contain my shock and rage and curtly cut off the self serving monologue. "What the fuck are you smoking? I ain't going to jail for you or any rotten outfit, company, whatever'!" I snapped with emphasis on the terms. "I'm out of here and headin' straight to the FBI."

"Thank God, Pearl's at lunch or it would be over right now," Barrow said about Pearl Jackson, his secretary. "Easy, Tom, easy. Please give me just ten minutes. The FBI can wait ten minutes."

I knew that it was a huge error but weakened, "It's one-twenty; you're on the clock."

"First, it's virtually foolproof. If I didn't drop the files on your desk, neither you or the FBI or even God Himself could have broken it. It's so simple that it borders on perfect." He paused for another cough break.

I was still enraged, "That god damned barking is on your time. So, it's `perfect' or what were the operative words `…borders on perfect'? `Borders on', I don't like at all. "

Barrow was back in control of his breathing. "In a nutshell, the Native Corporations in Alaska don't have to compete for Corps or any other government contracts. They were screwed over so many times by whitey and his governments that even the Congress saw that it had to give them a break – with the help of huge pushes from lobbyists and pols.

"They rigged it so all the feds have to do is put out specs for what they need, and if the Alaskans can do the work, they just tell us they'll do it on a non-compete contract and for how much.

And, naturally, they can do it because all they have to do is sub the work to a competent company here in the lower forty-eight – a company that just happens to have our fox in the henhouse - and it's a done deal.

"The company does the job, turns out a quality product – with a fifty percent markup over what it costs, including a fat profit for the natives, and we split the difference. Callahan approved the all invoices, and I counter signed them. They're paid and the files fly like migrating birds to some salt mine storage facility in the Midwest to disintegrate into dust over the next ten thousand years, no fuss, no muss, no nothing. That's it; it's that simple and that secure. Fred and I were into it for well over a couple of million each and we were lining up a whale that makes those numbers look like petty cash. And there's a full share in it for you. Well?"

"Well fucking what? You say it's safe, and I'm supposed to say, `Count me in.' You're joking, right?" I checked my watch and snapped, "On that three minute monologue, I'm supposed to bet – what twenty years in a federal can?" I yelled, paused and added, "Oh, and my family and everything else of value in my life? As far as I'm concerned this is a no go from the get go, and I'm out of here and on my phone."

I rose from my chair with a great show of disdain for Barrow, "You got anything more?" I asked very loudly.

Barrow coughed out, "Yes."

"What?"

"Yes, I have more. I didn't get into this for my health. There is one smart and mean son of a bitch running this show. Let me put it another way; I have weaknesses, and he exploited them. Like you, I'm not a real crook by nature, but he knew just how to turn me. He's like a matador observing the tendencies of the bull before the fight. When he gets into the ring, it's not even close to a fair fight. He blackmailed me and I fell in line. I'm really sorry and ashamed, but what could I do? ...Beyond satisfying my wildest dreams of avarice - times ten over."

Suddenly, I felt that I'd taken a powerful punch to my gut, "What do you mean by `mean son of a bitch'? Are you talking in riddles? Has he physically threatened you?"

A light went on in my head, and I asked, "Are you trying to say something about Fred Callahan's death?"

He reacted angrily, "I never said anything like that – or implied it. It was an accident. I asked directly and he guaranteed me that it was. I'd have turned him in myself if it wasn't."

I laughed in his face and said, "Tell me that's a fucking joke. You suspected that he killed your best friggin' friend, and you asked the `mean son of a bitch' himself - who just happen to have you by the balls and who you're obviously shittin' your pants in fear of - if he did Fred in, and he said, `No' and that was good enough for you. Is that about it?" as I guffawed my insult directly into his face once more.

After another purple faced contortion of coughing, Barrow acknowledged the weakness of his position with a lowering of his eyes and said so quietly that I could barely make it out, "You have to understand. We have to trust each other. We're in this together. But he is menacing, Tom. I don't know if twenty years in prison is right about these kinds of frauds, but it's a long time and he has no intention of pulling it."

"You ought to quit those weeds. They'll kill you," I said malevolently.

"There are worse ways to go. I don't drink and nicotine is the perfect drug for uptight felons."

"What? So if I buy in, it's booze or butts to get me through the day? This is the best you can do for why I should buy into this almost sure thing?"

By this point, I noticed that Barrow was being more aggressive and was beginning to push back on me.

"Maybe, but let me break it to you; it was no accident that you were selected for this offer. The matador-in-chief gave you a hard look before deciding you were partner material."

"What the hell are you saying? And cut the god damned riddles; speak English."

"None of this is my doing, but he's got big barbed hooks in your hide already and if my pitch doesn't work, hold your breath because he's going to set them – hard! First, he thinks you're smart enough to see the beauty of the scheme. And…and he's been setting you up for months."

My mind was racing madly, and before Barrow could go on, I said, "Roby!"

"See! Our leader knows partner material when he sees it. He's…"

I cut him off. "My trip?...The girl?"

"No matter what you're thinking, I'm sure that she found you attractive and that it wasn't all business," he said with an overly solicitous smile.

My heart sank, "New Orleans?"

"You get a gold star for that one too. Even before that."

"What else?"

"Don't make me go through it. I didn't do it or have anything to do with it, and I didn't want to be the messenger."

"Hey, you're the guy wearing the fucking mail man costume; I want it from the beginning. Now!"

"First, what I said about Fred and me picking you out of the crowd was true and had nothing to do with how the rest of this goes down. We saw you taking over the division when the dust settled and we quit – retired.

"When Fred was killed that created a vacancy that had to be filled or we were not only out of business but in deep trouble. Half the deliverables on our biggest contract to that point were in and paid, and there was no way we could complete the contract without somebody new - and quickly, too. Stopping in the middle of a contract would surely draw the bloodhounds and blow up the whole thing.

"I swear to God, Tom, I had nothing to do with it. Elmer Gantry and Sister Falconer wanted to see the personnel files on all of the contracting officers in the division so that they could take their pick among them. I swear that I had no choice but to deliver 'em. So…"

"Who? What the hell are you saying? Can't you ever stop with the fuckin' riddles?"

"I'm sorry, but this isn't easy for me. You may not be a reader, but did you ever see the movie, *Elmer Gantry?* Elmer and Sister Falconer were the lead characters and were the names Fred and I tagged our friends from McLean – when they were out of ear shot. A cynical thieving bastard and a screwball saint, they're perfect for running the company, and they match the movie. "

"For the record, just because I'm an accountant doesn't mean that I can't fucking read. I've loved reading since I was a kid and took all my humanities requirements in English and history. I've seen the Gantry flick a couple of times. I may be an ignoramus to you, but I'd appreciate it if you'd fake it and pretend that I'm not a complete moron...at least while you're trying to make the biggest fucking sale of your life."

"I'm sorry, Tom. You're right; I was out of line - and not at a good time. And I really do consider you to be a very intelligent person," he said. "Up on the tundra near Nome, Matt and Amanda are gods, very shrewd gods. They more than tithe from our profits; a full partnership is siphoned off into a company foundation for villages all over Alaska. They go up every summer and drop hundred dollar bills all across the bush: steel buildings for community centers and gyms, books for kids, icons of themselves for those who don't know the Russians left a couple of hundred years ago, whatever it takes to have the elders eating out of their hands and lining up with Matt to become Corps contractors.

"I'm telling you, Tom, the Robys return more to the native corporations than half the legitimate charities working up there, but, of course, there's one minor difference: It's not his dough, it's Uncle Sam's.

"This is one clever and mean couple; cross 'em at your peril."

"Stow the warning baloney and get back to how they're trying to hook me."

"Simple. They had me bring them a list of our contacting officers, and they took one look at it and spotted your name right away. I confirmed that you graduated from West Springfield High School, and Amanda went on and on about how you used to eat out of her hand in school. Old Elmer started casting the line right there. The rest you can figure."

"What have they got?" I said and paused before adding, "As if I can't guess."

"Do I have to?" Barrow begged.

I felt my quads tighten and I got ready to go over the desk and throttle the son of bitch, "Not if you don't mind doing a perp walk out of here in about ten minutes."

"Remember, you asked for it: your report on Cancun; a copy of the company check paying for it – that you signed very clearly and a disk of pretty graphic video images just waiting to be posted on the internet, and, naturally, with hard copies for your wife and folks – and the FBI and federal prosecutors. I've got copies for you sitting in my bottom drawer."

"You've seen the video?"

After another spasm, he said, "No. I've got the disk in an envelope, but I'm not into that kind of stuff… But Matt made a point of saying that the action is mighty hot…Oh, he also said that the sound track added to it."

I was pounding my right fist into my left hand. The pressure that had been building in my stomach was beginning to burn white hot. The acid was definitely potent enough to bore through the concrete and lead lining of a nuclear power plant. I almost cried as I thought, 'God damn, an asshole who can't even make out in a whore house with an unlimited Master Card screws a ten on the first date - and never smells a rat; real partner material, I'd say. Son of a bitch, I've got to get my head around this crap.' "I need to think."

"Take your time; there's no rush – for the next couple of days," Barrow said; his sarcasm was obvious.

"That's the whole pitch; our lives are in your hands until you make your call. You want the envelope? I'm sure they have the originals of everything," Barrow said as he reached in his drawer and pulled out a swollen eight by ten manila envelope and held it out for me.

I snatched it with a violent grab, turned toward the door and snarled, "You prick!"

THIRTEEN

I was back at my desk sorting out my options but going out for a drink and taking up cigarettes again kept interrupting my logic train. As I fantasized about heroically busting up the gang and explaining my motivation to the Washington Post, Barrow walked in and closed the door behind him.

"I've got a couple more points. May I sit down?"

"If you must; you still have five minutes left on your clock."

He pulled my visitor's chair up close and spoke softly, "I swear to God, Tom, it was never my intention to involve you in this mess. Fred and I honestly identified you as the comer among the young guys in the division, and we saw you taking over the division after we closed down the operation and left."

"Now why doesn't that make me want to thank you and dear old Fred for your good intentions regarding my future? And how has that noble statement changed my situation?" I asked in my smarmy best.

"I don't blame you for being upset; I'd be if I were in your shoes. But much as I said in my office, there are points I didn't get to make that you should consider while weighing your options – and mine. If you blow the whistle on us, it won't turn out like you're thinking right now, guaranteed. It…"

"And of course you know what I'm thinking," I snapped, cutting him off.

"Maybe. I was once in your spot and had to weigh everything. I chose the other way – with a lot of regret, but in thinking about it before and after the fact and over a long period, I want to make a couple of points, if you're open to listening."

"I haven't finished dialing 911 – but I'm on the last `1' and my finger's twitching."

"You may not believe this but you're going to be wrong no matter what you decide. Everybody extols whistle blowers when something big like this goes down, but, believe me, it's phony adulation. When it comes to rewarding the `snitch', it's an altogether different story.

"A rat is always a rat. Hard to believe, eh? You're thinking pure thoughts of how you're doing your patriotic duty, and two years from now when some boss is selecting someone to fill a job you want and it's between you and Joe Blow, a little bird will perch on Mr. Big's shoulder and whisper, `Hey, Phelan was the rat who outed those crooks in contracts. Do you need him sniffing around your shop? Don't you think Blow might be the safer choice, more cooperative?' And more times than not, old Blow gets the job. Trust me."

"Yeah, you've earned it. All I see in front of me is a frightened fraud making up – on the friggin' fly - all kinds of reasons why I shouldn't turn his thieving ass in."

"You're right. I'm frightened and deserve your contempt, and yes, it's mostly because of my self-interest. I'm scared close to death by my-self interest. But I've thought about this conversation for weeks, knowing it was going to take place long before you did. I also knew that despite my conflict of interest and despite the fact that I played a role in roping you into it, I really didn't do any of it with animosity toward you."

"Well thank God for that. I wouldn't want to be contemplating twenty years in prison because the guy who turned me into a criminal intended bad things for me."

He ignored the nasty crack and continued, "I've been watching you for a couple of years and pretty well knew that, with the hand you'd been dealt, you weren't the happiest clam in the division. I knew that your ambition was too great for the career track that you're on. And, while I know that everything I say is repelling to you at this moment, this is not only a way out of your various dilemmas but a way to another world."

"You got that right; a friggin' world where my boyfriend, Bubba, and I contemplate who gets the lower bunk for making whoopee."

He managed a weak laugh. "Yeah, that one too, but not really. It's a world of power, money and privilege beyond anything you've ever dreamed.

"If you drop the dime on me and even if it turns out just the way you're fantasizing, the best you can ever hope for is to move into my office and pull twenty-five years in my chair supervising instead of doing – what I know you despise. You'll inherit my office, chair, desk and credenza, and all of them are better than yours. Inviting, huh?"

"OK, I'll bite; what's the other world about?"

"All societies and groups are binary, no, actually ternary: us and them – and the rest; reds, whites and pinks; liberals, conservatives and moderates; all of them from the beginning of time till the end. And if you haven't figured it yet, American society is divided into three major groups: the haves, the have nots and, biggest of all, the working stiffs in the middle. But even if you divide those that work into their three compartments, you're still in the middle of the liberals and conservatives. Do you get what I just said?"

Without waiting for my answer, he pushed on. "That other world – the one I'm trying to guide you toward - is the small world of capitalism, the haves. It's all about money and the ability to control it; to move it so people will do what you think is best. It provides the power and the ability to have people do what you say. To have workers jump at your requests and never think about making demands, now that's satisfying."

Barrow stopped and looked me in the eye and waited for my reaction. When I said nothing, he went on with his tale, "I don't have what it takes, Tom. Money bores me, seriously, and, at heart, I'm lazy. Fred Callahan, much as I liked him, was a small time thinker. He was venal, saw his chances and took them. He drove expensive cars, took nice vacations, bought bobbles for his wife and even got buried in the most expensive casket on the East Coast."

"But I'm different, a man of quality, a great man just ready to blossom," I offered sarcastically.

He smiled. "You took the words right out of my mouth."

He became deadly serious again, "But even though I might have been smart enough to see that I was just a grunt, a nobody, like when I was an infantry platoon leader in Vietnam and since then as a worker in the government, it was clear to me that I was nothing but a wage slave or, as the old Greeks used to say of their slaves: just tools with life in them.

"No, I was really just a computer chip with life in it to the staff officers in Nam and to the smart guys at the Pentagon, the White

House, and to all the Washington everybody thinks and dreams about. But I'm a human being and can see clearly what they think of me."

I was shocked. "Boy, you are one angry bastard and I never had an inkling of it until this minute."

"Maybe you're right, but I don't see it that way. I see it as finally being onto the system. And even if it's true, maybe it's you who should be angry out of your mind.

"With your brains and a little money, I'm convinced that you can move in the circles I'm talking about. Roby's smart and ruthless, but not smart enough, and he has to be controlled or he'll bring the house down on us. He'll never be able to stop. You're the missing piece, Tom, the missing link."

"You must really think I'm stupid; that two or three million bucks would make me a Rockefeller or Warren Buffet. That's small time dough when it comes to the games you're bullshitting about.

"Everything you're saying is nothing but self-serving bullshit."

"You're absolutely right; it is self-serving bullshit begging you not to drop your dime on me, but that's not all it is. It's also the truth. It isn't the two or three or five million; it's what you could leverage it into. Roby's project in Mexico could launch you into the top ranks of the hospitality or gaming businesses. It's not what you have but what you control. The cynics call it `OPM', other people's money, but the correct term is leverage. It's a term that's in bad repute in the face of this terrible recession, but it's the secret to the system – always was and always will be.

"Think about it. Toss that green eye shade the Corps issued you when you came aboard and think about how you could leverage four or five million dollars. There are possibilities beyond all of your dreams. You're children could go to Ivy League colleges. You could buy into banks, whatever; just unleash your imagination."

"But my ticket to that bullshit world you're selling is for me to be a crook. Right?"

"You're a real innocent, Phelan. Are you really so naïve as to think that all of the elites got there following the Golden Rule? Surely you're not that stupid or foolish. Have I overestimated you that badly?"

Recognizing the precariousness of my position, I said nothing.

After a pause and a smile, Barrow continued, "That world is there to be taken. How you get to it is up to you. Turn us in and go invent a computer operating system, start a billion dollar hedge fund, break the bank of England – if you can. All I'm saying is that it's there. I know a way in and I can help you.

"I didn't say you could be as famous as Bill Gates; most of the wealthy and powerful people aren't. But they control massive shares of the wealth of the country – all the while leading quiet, privileged lives.

"And as I said before, no matter what you do, you're wrong; being in the wrong place at the wrong time means that your roads into that other world have changed dramatically. You never saw a way before, but you could have started that hedge fund that you're only now coming to recognize. My guess is that like the vast majority of people you never even suspected there was another way of life open to you.

"Oh, I know I'm trying to stay out of prison, but I'm also willing to give you something to avoid it, something big, a chance."

He paused for a moment and said, "There's more, but my ten minutes are up and I've had most of my say. But as Robert Frost pointed out, `Two roads diverged in a yellow wood, and sorry I could not travel both...'

"You're at that fork, Tom. You can be my accuser or you can move into that other world.

"If you cross over, it'll be morning in America again – for you and yours. You'll be in the Capitalist Club and you get to choose your side of the aisle when you get there. You can be an Ayn Rand Objectivist self made asshole and live like some of the heavies in The Great Gatsby; you can be like most sensible wealthy people, quietly travelling the world and attending musicals on Broadway and in London and otherwise enjoying the fruits of their labor; or, in your case – if your guilt is too heavy – you can become a liberal and a philanthropist and assuage your guilt by sharing your ill gotten gains with the downtrodden. But it's up to you; you'll be in the capitalist world and you get to choose among three new doors.

"I'm sure what you'll find if you pass through the magic portal is that, as in all groups, those on the right can hardly bear the sight of the left wingers and vice versa, but that despite all the animosity they fully accept the standing of the other. The lefties, for all their love of the unwashed, stand side by side with their fraternal brothers on the right when their privileges are threatened.

"Well that's my spiel; give me a heads up on your choice, if you can."

Barrow rose and walked slowly out, closing the door behind him.

"Shit! This is too much for little Tommy Phelan," I whispered.

FOURTEEN

Hunkered down behind my closed office door, I fingered the copy of the check for several seconds before tossing it on the desk. Pulling the copy of my report to Roby from the manila envelope, I read the first two paragraphs and whispered, "Now that's fine shit…for setting up a stupid Irishman like Tommy Phelan."

Reaching into the envelope again, I pulled out the disk. Gazing at it, I thought, `What if I smashed it? The end of it?' "Not likely, asshole!" I said in a loud voice that frightened me. "You stupid shit, why don't you just post it for the whole damn division to see?" I hissed in a whisper.

I pushed the button to open my computer. "What happens in Cancun stays in Cancun; right, bright boy?

"At least there's one consolation: the bitch definitely told Roby that she found me attractive. That's what that cowardly moron told me, right?" I said, laughing softly at the irony of the beautiful trap they'd caught me in.

I pushed the button again. "I can't look at that shit… with friggin' sound yet.

"Well, are you in or out?"

I closed my eyes, 'Let's see; the downer who smelled out those phony Robys and kept telling you that their odor was rotten turns out to be the one person in the world who had your interests at heart. Yep, clearly a downer who wasn't smart enough to see the big picture. Man how blind? How fucking dumb? Their whole friggin' world – built on shit. And you couldn't wait to wallow in it with them. Way to go, Tommy.

'No more Chevys for you, Tommy Phelan. Oh no, you're a Beamer man now. And that shitty little ranch in that cheek by jowl subdivision…yeah that place where the residents aren't smart enough to follow you to the big time and all they can do is love you…yeah, that shack ain't nearly nice enough for you, Tommy boy. No siree, a man with your brains, talent and really great character should be living in McLean…or Georgetown.'

"OK moron, let's go over that cost benefit analysis one more time," I whispered as the scenarios began to scroll before my closed eyes. `One: dive into the pool and find twenty years in the pen; lose the only people on the planet who give a crap whether you live or die; disgrace the folks who taught you right from wrong… That's all? Ha!

'Not too hot.

'Dos: blow the whistle; be the rat; win a divorce from the only girl who ever loved you and bet on you…That's all?…Oh, yeah, and be sure to look both ways before you cross Jeff Davis Highway.

'Verdict: another loser.'

'Or, tres: dive into that same pool and get away with it; get rich; buy a place overlooking the Potomac… with parking for your two shiny E – Class Mercedes sedans - you are after all, just a regular guy at heart; buy into a thriving business; and live happily ever after.'

'Three sounds good. But, hey, ain't that the same as number one that got you a room for two in the old Gray Bar Motel? Depends on your perspective; is that pool half full or half empty? Oh yeah, but what about the window treatments? Barred windows or Belgian lace?'

I whistled silently and whispered, "Houston, we have a problem, make that `problems'."

Carefully placing the poison pills back in the envelope, I dropped the package into my canvas satchel and announced the rest of my schedule, "Man, I need a Manhattan… or two or three; but no more friggin' tequila for you, asshole."

FIFTEEN

My head was still aching as I plopped into my chair the following morning. Barrow saw me enter and chased after me like an anxious real estate agent who thinks he's on the verge of losing a deal.

Shutting the door behind him, and in an obvious state of high anxiety, he asked, "Are you on board?"

"No, but you're still here, so don't get your ass all worked up just yet."

Barrow bristled, "Hey, you can't talk to me like that. I'm still the boss around here."

"No, asshole, I'm the fuckin' boss around here, at least till I decide what happens to you. And when I do decide, you're either a perp or my partner; the friggin' partner who ruined my useless rotten life.

"My head's killing me. I haven't decided anything. Consider yourself lucky that nobody's punched you in the fuckin' nose or that your hands aren't cuffed behind your back."

I let out a huge sigh and said in a far more conciliatory manner, "I know that you're screwed, too, John," but almost instantly my tone shifted back to that inspired by the rage that was consuming me. "No doubt, my feelings are gonna change no matter what happens, but right now, I don't want to say another damn word about how I feel about you. Honest to God, I can't stand the fucking sight of you, so slink your ass out of here and leave me alone to feel sorry for myself. Now!"

With amazing speed and balance, Barrow pirouetted and flew out the door with the quickness and agility of a squirrel deciding he'd chosen the wrong moment to cross the road, the sallow face and racking cough completely absent as he scurried to his office.

Two hours and three coffees later, I walked into Barrow's office and closed the door. "I've got questions."

John leaped up. "Sit down; I'll do my best," he said looking like one of the waiters at The Prime Rib, bowing and scraping obsequiously.

My nerves were completely frazzled, but I had fight to suppress a smile as I watched him squirm. "Easy, John, I ain't going to pop you one in the snoot; that notion's past."

"I know how you feel, Tom, I really do. I was in your spot a couple of years ago, and I was so damn angry at Fred. Imagine, my best friend setting me on this horrible path; I could have shot him on the spot.

"I don't want to rile you up any more, but I had it even worse. Remember, we're now in the middle of the mess, and when Fred was killed we had to lean on you – or someone else in the division – or we were caught dead to rights.

"When they nailed me, it was the front end of the deal. They came after me with a vengeance when they never had to; it was the beginning and they were in no danger. It..."

"You're breaking my fuckin' heart, John; you had it so much worse than I do."

"I'm sorry. I'm so frightened that I can't think straight," he said with a groan before going on. "And understand my nerves. I'm laying life on the line with you. At this minute, my future is in your hands."

"Don't start with that whining shit!" instantly I was at my boiling point, "This is my time, and I need answers for my butt, not yours."

"Sorry; shoot."

"I don't have my gun." I deadpanned.

He laughed nervously, leading to another spasm of coughing.

"Explain to me again how nobody gets to audit what Fred signed off on and that you approved."

"It's not that they can't, but there's a hole in the system as big as the Grand Canyon and nobody's charged with filling it. And there's no incentive for anyone to look. Once I sign off, the package heads for Finance for routine payment and then flies off to the salt mine's dead letter file with a `do not disturb' sign. I've signed off on dozens of invoices and haven't had to answer a single question about any of them – not one.

"Nobody cares one iota. It's a perpetual motion money machine. A request for proposal is issued by one of our operating divisions and Fred alerts Roby – or used to. A bid floats in from a Native Corporation with the work to be done by a competent contractor here in the area. The division signs off and Callahan approves it. I sign off, a contract is issued and the work is done – competently. An invoice is submitted and Callahan and I sign off once more. Lo and behold, a check soars like the American eagle to the contractor and the company issues its own checks to our dummy corporations, and before you know it boxes of almost new Ben Franklins appear miraculously at the partners' drops.

"It's that simple, and it's `almost' perfect... and nobody gives a damn."

I saw John's confidence rise. He was talking faster and he was smiling as he described the beauty of the operation. I could tell that like any good salesman he was sold on his own product and was fast closing the deal.

"Roby's smart. Fred watched him like a hawk. Every payment to us is rounded up to the next hundred. He's got a laundry – that I really know nothing about - that can produce cash in a flash. Our check to the company goes out in the mail, and two weeks later wrapped, randomly numbered hundreds arrive. Roby's got it so that the discount on the cash is just twenty-five percent. So if the invoice is for a hundred thousand, you get seventy-five percent of one sixth of that. Both Fred and I thought that was damn good since that means there's no paper trail connecting us to the company.

Callahan counted every single packet and they were always perfect. Honor among thieves to the nth degree.

"Remember I told you about *Elmer Gantry*?"

"So?"

"There was another old movie, *The Lady Killers*, an old black and white that was shot long before your time; well the gang got away with the caper when the old lady who was perpetually ratting them out was finally told by the cops, "Hey, it's just insurance company money they ripped off. The policy's been paid; nobody cares. The old lady shakes her head and it fades to black.

"Tom, this is ten times better than insurance dough; it's federal money. Got it, Tom? It isn't real money; it's federal money. But when it hits your doorstep, it's real; it's a miracle - transubstantiation in action, Monopoly money to federal etchings. Those are real hundred dollar bills; neat, randomly numbered, wrapped, counted - and most important - yours by the bucket full. It's the miracle of the loaves and fishes, federal style.

"Our lives have been transformed, Tom, and nobody's the wiser – or hurt. Don't miss the tide, Tom, don't miss it. It goes out in just days and we're riding it or we get eaten by alligators here in the shallows."

I snapped at him, "No, John, at this point you're looking at the inside of the alligator; I'm not part of the `we'.

"You said there was tension between Callahan and Roby; why?"

"I don't know how direct it was; I never saw them together. But Fred was unhappy with the split. It was all his idea but all he got was one sixth of the proceeds. He was always grousing to me about Roby getting three full shares.

"I tried to calm him down by explaining that one of the shares was being spread around the Alaskan native villages as a come on; another covered all the other costs; and last was Roby's own. But despite knowing that, Fred knew it was all his idea and he was always angry about it."

I asked as sincerely as I could, "Do you really think the Callahan hit was an accident?"

Barrow coughed and blurted out, "I think about it a lot, but right now I'm leaning to the notion that it was an accident and I don't think Roby had anything to do with it. Fred's death put us in this hole, and if you think Roby was looking forward to going through this trauma with you, you're crazy.

"Besides, Roby's a sneaky crook, but I doubt that he could be a killer. Like the rest of us, Matt fell into this; he's no gangster. I find it hard to believe that he'd ever take a chance and drive a car over Fred. And just think it through, if he contracted the job; those things don't work; then there's another crook with something on him and a car with dents and blood.

"Trust me; Matt's as paranoid as the rest of us. You think he's up to strangling somebody or driving into 'em? No way! It would take the best detail man in Virginia to clean up the crap in his car. Knowing Roby the way I do, none of it makes sense.

"But he's a mean bastard with millions of bucks and his freedom at stake, so you never really know, and paranoia isn't necessarily the same thing as fear. I'm sure that he likes it that we might be sweating over whether he was up to knocking us off. But still my bottom line guess is that it was what it was, a simple hit and run. As long as Fred was doing the job, I think Roby was willing to put up with his bitching."

"That's it! Not another word; I have to think." Rising and leaving Barrow's office as if John wasn't even there, I added, "I still need more time."

I was getting crazier by the minute, and I had to decide – soon.

SIXTEEN

"**O**f course you're a good guy, Tommy. What's got into you? You've been acting very strange lately. You feelin' OK?" Jen asked, anxiety written all over her face.

"I'm fine. I just need you to say that I'm pulling my weight. Jeez, you're busting your hump around here twenty-four seven, and all I do is keep up with the Redskins and Orioles.

"It seems like we've been playing the barefoot and pregnant routine forever, and I see you working non-stop, and me, just fartin' around, gettin' nowhere. Christ I can't even cut the grass without complaining," I said, looking down at the table.

"Are you happy, Jen. I mean `really happy'?"

"What's eating you, Tommy? You havin' trouble at work?"

"No, no. With the baby almost here and you still workin' like a dog, I just get feelin' like I'm not treatin' you right is all."

"I'm fine, Tommy. You're a good father and a true blue husband. I wouldn't trade you in on anybody. I don't pine for things, hon. I've got what I wanted all along. Sure it's rough weighing thirty pounds more than normal but look at what's causing it," she said with a big grin while pointing to the basketball under her smock.

"Life's good. I've got you; we've got each other. We have the best little kids in the world, and in a few days or weeks, we'll triple our pleasure," she said with a happy laugh before going on with, " We have a new house. You're doing great. What more could I want?"

I tried to pull myself together, "Nothing, Baby, nothin'. I must be blind not to see that I've got the world by the ass," I said with a smile and reached to envelop her in a gentle bear hug.

The next morning, closing the door behind me, I stood straight as an arrow in front of Barrow's desk. "I know this is becoming a soap opera, but I've still got things to clear up."

"Not a problem. Sit down and let's see if I can handle them," he offered like an old country doctor, a phony old country doctor.

"The truth is I've never committed a felony in my life, and I don't want to start now. I have to know; are you taping these sessions with me?"

"What? Are you nuts? That'd be crazy, Tom. Why…"

My response was emitted as if from a fire hose, "I know it's crazy, but I'm friggin' crazy out of my fucking mind. I want a direct answer. But before that, I want you to know that I've never threatened anybody since I was in the second grade and that was to push a little shit of a girl down in the grass, but – listen, listen up - if it turns out that that there's a record of our talks, regardless of whether it hurts me or not, I swear to God, I'm going to kill you. I…"

"For the love of God, Tom, tone it down; Pearl will hear you," he begged, "Easy does it, you're being hysterical, way over-agitated; you have to relax – at least a little. I know that you don't mean what you're saying and that you're feeling just like I did when I got trapped into this. I'm not in this to hurt you; you have to believe that. I'm a victim just like you. I swear I'm not wearing a wire or doing anything else to record what we're saying. I'm not.

"Come on, sit down. Calm down and give me a shot at easing your mind."

I fought the urge to bolt and after shifting my weight a half a dozen times like a little kid with a real bad need to pee, I finally settled into the chair.

"Good man; now what else is bothering you?"

"Tell me all about the operation. How'd you get caught up in it?"

"As I said, Fred cracked the code on the scheme and, in fact, the night he was killed he told me that he had it figured two or three years before we started. Over the years he became convinced that we could get away with it. He…"

"…was a friggin' crook," I interrupted.

"Ah, come on, Tom, cut me some slack; you want answers but now you're acting like a kid. Sure he was a crook, if that's what you have to hear, but it's never that easy. He just let it lay like a ten carat diamond sitting in the gutter that he passed every day for years. There's an old line from Tammany Hall – the old New York City political machine – that…"

"I goddamn well know what Tammany Hall was. Jesus, you talk to me like I'm a friggin' stupid bumpkin."

"I'm sorry; you're right. But the line still fits and rings true in a lot of situations, 'I seen my opportunities and I took 'em,' You know, Tom, gold bullion just sitting unattended in plain sight could blind a lot of guys and make their fingers sticky. Easy for you and me; we're holier than Fred, but we didn't see the diamond or the bullion just sitting there waiting for us.

"The Fred I once knew was a better Christian than I and – maybe even you – at least I thought he was and he belonged to some men's group in his parish up in Springfield. Roby was fresh out of law school and was trolling for wills and trusts and joined Fred's group looking for small scores.

"I don't know which of 'em was the chicken or which the egg, but somehow they got to talking and ultimately Fred laid it out for Matt who saw the beauty of it instantly – it was hard not to – and over time and jacking each other up over it, they decided that they could make it work.

"It was obvious that they needed me, but they let that go till they set up the outside stuff. Matt found a contractor who could do big information tech jobs that had a guy in the accounting department with larceny in his heart –that's Johnston. You've seen his name in the files?"

"Yeah," I said.

"I've never met the guy. Roby keeps everything compartmentalized, so that, too, works in our favor when it comes to security. I'm pretty sure…maybe I'm just hoping…that Johnston doesn't know my name, not that it makes a hell of a lot of difference if the FBI gets wind of it.

"Anyway, they found a small IT request for proposal from our electronics guys and connected up one of the Alaskan Native corporations with Johnston's company and set up a legitimate bid. Naturally, we gave it to them – everybody, including me, innocent me, signed off, and it went like clockwork.

"So it was time to set me up; they did, and in just a few weeks we were in business. It was a simple as that, and it works. We…"

I broke in, "How'd they get to you? I have to know."

Barrow was overcome by one of his coughing spells before being able to respond, "I…Don't go that way. I can't…I won't say…I won't. I'll just say that it wasn't far different from what happened to you, but I… I have other weaknesses, too. I like nice things, especially art, and I'm too lazy or not smart enough to… to…figure out how to acquire them. Roby's a fine judge of horse flesh and it didn't take a lot of his wattage to figure a way to marry desire and inability, and I was onboard as partner. I can't tell you the torment…"

Barrow took time for another coughing spell before saying, "In any event, that was it. I was in, loaded with shame and self loathing, but in."

"I'm sorry," I said. "But if that prick thinks I'm signing off on one friggin' invoice without guarantees, he's friggin' nuts.

"If I was to come aboard – and I ain't saying I am - I'd need a signing bonus. I'd have to have a hundred thousand bucks – cash – in advance; no ands, ifs or buts. You hear me?" I said barely below a shout.

"Jesus, Tom, Pearl's right outside the door! I get you loud and clear. I'll bag it myself and deliver it within forty-eight hours. That…"

"Bullshit! I don't want it from you. I want you to put it right to Roby and have him get it done. I ain't shittin', John; I'm scared to death. It's got to be that way or it's no way," I said, feeling sweat rings wicking under both arms.

"Take it easy; I get what you're going through."

He went on, "Settle down. That's reasonable reaction and a non-problem. I'll call Roby, and I guarantee that it will be done, guarantee it. You'll see; we can make things happen."

"And I want to meet with the bastard. I want to face down the son-of-a-bitch and let him know what I think of him for this whole fucking mess. How he's ruining my whole fucking life. How…"

"Easy, Tom. Think about it; that'll never fly. You've got him by the balls, and he'll never meet with you until you're onboard.

This is like the Cold War; you've got him by the short hairs but he hasn't got an equal lock on yours, so he sure as hell won't enter disarmament talks till there's mutually assured destruction. Know what I mean?"

I watched nervously as Barrow smiled slightly, apparently liking his MAD analogy.

Later that same afternoon, I was at my desk nervously drinking coffee when Barrow entered. "How many coffees have you had?"

"Too damn many. What you got?"

"Just as I thought, Roby had a string of four letter expletives for your demand to see him before you're onboard. But he bit on the signing bonus like a hungry bass rising for a good lure. Can you get out of the house Saturday morning?"

"So I don't get to knock the bastard's teeth out," I said through a widening smile. "Oh, well…"

Barrow didn't say a word as he waited for my real decision.

The tension rose until I relented with, "I'm sure…sure. I need to get some junk at the hardware store. I can get out."

John became animated and spoke rapidly, "Go to Fair Oaks Mall; there's an area in the mall just behind the Starbucks stand with a lot of easy chairs and sofas. Pick a seat with a space between you and the next chair or sofa and sit down. Read something, anything – like you're waiting while your wife shops. A woman carrying a couple of Lord &Taylor shopping bags will sit next to you and rest the bags next to her seat – and yours. After a few minutes, she'll get up and leave taking one of the bags – the other's your signing bonus and welcome wagon greeting.

"Be cool; wait a couple of minutes and then very casually be on your way, but with the bag. When you get to a secure place, open it, count it, do whatever you want with it. We'll expect you on Monday morning, partner."

"John, I'm really crapping my drawers."

He smiled, coughed and said, "Like I said, Tom, it borders on perfect."

I reacted angrily, "This is no time for shitty jokes. This is way worse than anything I've ever done in my life – and a hell of a lot more dangerous."

"I'm sorry. It was just too tempting. You're going to have to settle down; you look like you've been hit by a bus."

"But I'm not dying of tuberculosis like you," I said malevolently as he rose to leave.

It was a hot and muggy Saturday, the second in July, and I watched the frumpy middle aged woman walk away and thought, 'That's the first normal looking woman connected with Roby I've come across.' As I casually turned, I saw the handles of the shopping bag above the wings of my chair and was filled with dread. 'My God, if I pick that up…twenty fucking years.'

Checking my watch, I thought I'd wait one more full minute before picking up the bag. Lifting my eyes, I was horrified as a middle aged man dropped into the chair next to me and placed his own bag from Macy's right next to mine. Panicking, I forgot my most recent decision and grabbed for my bag - obviously far too quickly - and departed at much too rapid a pace. I didn't dare to look back at the guy who must have wondered what the hell had happened.

Approaching my car at a near trot, I clicked open the trunk, tossed in the bag, slammed the lid and jumped in front. I was breathing heavily, "Oh, shit, that bastard has to have a video of the whole thing," I said aloud. "Easy, Tommy, boy, you are so goddamn paranoid and way beyond out of your mind."

Driving out of the mall onto Route 50, I eased the car quickly into the left turn lane for I-66 east toward Washington, but at the last possible instant, I swerved back into the Route 50 lane and checked my rear view mirror. "See, asshole, nobody's there. Ease up and drive home – at the speed limit."

Only as I approached Braddock Road did I recall my alleged primary mission and looped back to the mall. "You went to the hardware store, moron…I can get it at Sears. A life of friggin' crime is probably not the best career choice for a cowardly fool like you, Phelan."

Half an hour later, I pulled into our carport and thought, `If she comes out, I'm going to have to call 911 for the rescue squad.'

I flew from the car, grabbed the step ladder leaning against the wall and quickly opened the ceiling storage panel of the carport and raced down again to the trunk. Grabbing the bag, I scrambled to the overhead and tossed in the package. Closing the door, I realized that I hadn't been breathing and gasped my way to near normal respiration. `She sure as shit can't climb up there while she's built like a hippo.'

Attempting all the while to pull myself together, I opened the kitchen door and said as calmly as I could to Jen who was standing near the sink. "Hey, Babe, I'm back. How're you doing?"

"Tommy, it's time; I'm getting pains," she said with one hand on her belly and the other on the counter.

"Oh, shit! OK Hon, grab your bag. I'm already dialing Mom."

On Tuesday morning Barrow was waiting for me and I thought, 'Not bad; he's shittin' his pants but looking pretty cool for a guy strapped into the electric chair.'

"Good thing you called in about the baby yesterday, I'd have thought you were on your way to Brazil – or wherever else there's no extradition treaty with us."

"That's lame, John."

"How're they doing?"

"That's more like it. They're both fine; thanks. My mother's staying with them today. Jesus, they were home on Sunday; my mother couldn't believe how fast they get discharged these days. My daughter can't wait to hold him, and the boy's oblivious.

"Jen's mother is driving down from Pennsylvania tomorrow and staying for a week."

Barrow turned and quietly closed the door. "You got the goodies?"

"Just like you said, but I panicked and almost screwed up the whole thing."

"What happened?"

"Nothing, really, never mind, but I have to learn to be a cooler felon, like you."

I surmised that John didn't know whether to laugh or to snap at me. 'Fuck you!' I thought. 'You got me into this mess.'

"Did you count it? I told you it would be all there."

"No. With the baby and all, I had all I could do to get it out of sight."

"What's that mean?"

"Nothing. I'm in."

Barrow did a reverse of Dorian Grey's picture right before my eyes.

"I knew you were the right guy."

The soap opera was over. "Well thanks for the vote of confidence. Let me dig out my file. I'll sign the invoices and bring them right in," I said watching him depart doing his best imitation of Fred Astaire high stepping back to his hole. 'Made his friggin' day. Saved his useless life and fucked up mine forever.' I thought while honing my blame everybody else game.

The file was sitting on my gun metal gray credenza, and I plopped it on my desk. Opening the file, I stared at the stack of four invoices that had built up since Fred Callahan's ill timed death. Shuffling them, I placed the oldest in the center of my blotter. "Your first overt act as a felon – well maybe the second; you, Phelan, are signing your own arrest warrant.

"But I'm being blackmailed. BFD; this is nothing compared to what they did to Patty Hearst and they put that poor bitch in the slammer. Cut the shit and sign. Who are you trying to convince? Why Tommy Phelan, of course," I answered the question at the end of the soliloquy for myself and grabbed my government-issue pen and boldly signed my name. 'What the hell, I'm the gang's John Hancock,' as I finished with a flourish.

With the crime committed with full intent, I looked up honestly expecting to see the FBI bursting through the door. Waiting for almost a minute that seemed like ten, I sighed and affixed my name to the remaining invoices, far less flamboyantly.

About an hour after my histrionics, Barrow came in and shut the door. "Roby will meet you at two o'clock today in the main cafeteria of the National Gallery of Art – the one between the two wings. Pick out one of the small tables and have a coffee till he arrives," John announced. "Oh, and don't forget: you're now a partner."

"Should I take leave?"

"Hell no! I'll tell Pearl that I have a meeting at the Pentagon that I can't make and that you're going up in my place."

After lunch, I drove to Pentagon City and took a Metro train to the Gallery Place stop. Still paranoid, I turned around at every corner and light to check on whether I was being followed. 'Is it too late to return my purchase? You are one ridiculous basket case, Phelan. You're the most cowardly scoundrel ever.'

Instead of a coffee, I grabbed a beer and found a relatively lonely table at which to wait for my new boss. Seeing Roby coming through the checkout line, I perked up and forced myself to focus on the Metro Section of a copy of the Washington Post that had been left by a prior patron of the arts.

Roby sat down and in a very soft but forceful voice immediately sounded nasty and annoyed, "You wanted to meet; here I am. Just remember; you're in."

"I'm in and I'm done. What you did to me was rotten."

"I have some guilt...very damn little, but what the hell was I supposed to do? Invite you over to the house and spill the whole thing and help you dial 911?"

Getting over his slight case of angst quickly, Matt barked, "OK you've got a beef; get over it. You're an adult in full control of your faculties and with full intent, you did what it took. So..."

"I was entrapped and you black..."

"Hey, if it makes you feel better; sure I blackmailed you. It works for you and for me but guess again if you think that shit'll play for a jury. All you had to do was come clean with your wife about one friggin' sleazy weekend stand in which you were entrapped. Christ, half the guys in America have been caught in worse situations and the truly honest ones would have called the cops at the first whiff of corruption.

"Face it; what would have happened if you had just come clean? A few quarts of tears, some broken fucking crockery and a couple of weeks on the couch and you'd have been home free.

"Jesus, Tommy, Jen was blown up like a frigging hot air balloon with that baby, and you weren't getting anything anyway. And you had no choice? You're shitting me.

"So stop with the crap about being a friggin' virgin. If this show goes down - and trust me - it isn't going to happen – and you're not the rat, I'm a big boy and I'll take a slightly bigger share of the fall. I'll tell 'em – in great detail – how I made you screw the best looking broad in Mexico. Naturally I'll make them watch the video three or four times. By the way, you handled yourself a lot better than I thought you could. Your acrobatics at the beach under the palms were very impressive. Man, when you were in high school you couldn't walk and chew gum at the same time."

"I knew you were an asshole then and you still are," I said quietly but with barely controlled rage.

"And we're partners," Roby said with a smirk and continued, "What bullshit. Now get with the program; we're all gonna be rich," he said with a final flourish and a wide smile.

"John says it's been a soap opera down at Belvoir but that's over now. Right? We're a solid outfit, as professional as we can be at all times and that means you. Well?"

With only silence emanating from me, Matt continued, "Come on; did I twist your arm to pick up the bag or sign the fucking invoices?"

"The choice was clear: join or be ruined. That's entrapment and blackmail."

"Phelan, I'm going to sit through about another thirty seconds of your happy horseshit – I should say unhappy horseshit, and then I'm going into the gallery to improve my mind.

"The sooner you face the fact that you're a crooked bastard at heart, and that you're now a bona fide felon and no better than the rest of us, the better off we'll all be. Your damn waltz to a plea bargain that's never going to happen won't work with the FBI, or the prosecutors, or the jury or the judge, so just start working on getting rich and spending some of it. Maybe you should take another trip to Cancun; might do you good.

"By the way, if that deal in Cancun works and we're able to transition to the legitimate big time, despite these fucking stupid theatrics, you really can have that job managing the contract. That way you can bang your eyeballs out every quarter. She told me that she has a crush on you," he said with a huge guffaw and left me sitting at the table, stunned.

Roby's stride toward the West Building of the gallery was that of a war hero accepting a ticker tape parade down Broadway. Suddenly he stopped, wheeled about and charged back to the table. Sitting down again, he lowered his head and said softly but with cold efficiency, "Now that the melodrama is over, I have real business. I know that you'll survive this lecture and be stronger for it.

"We can't be seen together again, and, unless it's absolutely vital, we shouldn't even call each other. I don't speak to Barrow any more than I have to and then just for business. Let's keep communication to an absolute minimum and use him for a conduit unless it's vitally important for me to know it from you directly."

There seemed to be no need for a reply, but I blurted out, "Yeah, OK, right."

Matt rose again and walked casually away.

'Like I ever want to see you again, asshole,' I thought as I licked my wounds over my abysmal performance in the great confrontation. `Soap opera? You're shitting me! On The Young and the Restless, Victor Newman would have punched out your fucking lights and slammed a hundred million dollar Van Gogh over your friggin' head.'

SEVENTEEN

By Labor Day life at home and at the office had settled into routines only slightly different from those prior to the birth of Sean and my assuming the role of certifier in chief of fraudulent invoices. In practice my second job was that of just another bureaucrat reading and writing memos from nine to five, but truly I was enjoying the diversity of work as Barrow's special assistant compared to being simply a junior contracting officer.

In the process of reviewing a memo prepared by one of the branches for Barrow's signature, I was startled to find John standing in front of my desk. My door was closed and I went on full alert. "What's up?"

Barrow was a new man, far more confident than he'd been prior to my becoming a partner, and in a clear voice he said, "I passed the oldest Alaskan invoice to Finance the day you gave it to me and held the others back. I'll send them in about one a week until we're caught up.

"You have another date on Saturday... same place, same time, same MO, except it's a two bagger. Can you make it?"

"That's kind of public, don't you think? I pretty near blew the whole thing last time."

"I'm sure you'll be fine and nothing's better than a crowd. We change drops regularly but that one's still good for while. You're just going to have to get used to acting normally on pickup runs."

"You still sure you've made the right selection?" I said with a chuckle.

"Absolutely! Just get with the program. It's a lock and you're all in."

"Two bagger?"

"Wow! You're slow...too many Benjamins to fit in one bag. Capisce?"

"Of course! And what's with the `capisce'? Practicing your Mafia boss routine?"

His smile withered, "You've been around here long enough to know that guys have gone wrong for ten grand, five...even less than a thousand bucks. This is good and it's big and it won't blow up on us. Relax and start acting like everything's routine.

"Now answer my question; can you make your date?"

"Oh yeah, no problem."

I promised to keep my paranoia in check during the payroll exchanges. My performance during the first act was such a horrible display of cowardice and ineptitude that a repeat could actually be fatal for the enterprise – and, more important, for me personally. So that Saturday, while waiting in my easy chair in the mall, I tried to keep my eyes on the Tom Boswell column about the Redskins in the Washington Post. But I admitted failure as my continual peering over the masthead of the sports section to seek out my new girlfriend would clearly give me away to any lurking G-man. 'Head down, stupid shit.' With that internal admonition, my eyes focused back on football.

I felt but didn't see the woman slide the two bags in the space between the chairs and then sit down on my left. 'Don't look up, idiot!' I thought and was proud of my success. I was even happier when I noted her departure using only my peripheral vision. 'The Skins are going to stink again; got it. Good boy, Tommy; maybe you do have the makings of a real `made man.'

I rose casually, recovered my shopping bags and strolled through the mall and the J.C. Penney store to my trusty Malibu and coolly placed the bags in the trunk as if they were filled with pillows that Jen might well have sent me out to buy. As I turned from clicking my seat belt to checking the mirrors for FBI agents, I whispered, "Not bad. Now as the shepherd said when he heard the wolves howling, `Let's get the flock out of here'... but slowly."

Jen was back on her feet and showed almost no sign of being in recovery from childbirth, but my mother was still coming by almost every day to do the heavy work of the cleaning and cooking. So when I pulled up and saw the old steel gray beetle Caprice parked out front I wasn't surprised and made no effort to remove the packages from the car.

Inside, I greeted her, "Hey, Mom, how's it going?"

"Couldn't be better. I'm just finishing up. Jen and the baby are napping and the kids are downstairs watching cartoons. Now that you're here, I'm heading home. Dad's beginning to think that I've moved in here."

"Nothing too good for the blood, eh Mom? Tell Dad not to worry; I'll stop by some night after work and he'll get a real meal for a change."

Mom laughed and said, "You're so smart, but soon enough you'll find yourself being treated the same way unless you have a grandchild in tow. And – if you live to be his age - don't be surprised when you have the same complaints he has."

I kissed her and watched until her car disappeared. She had gone home without going downstairs to check on the Cartoon Network, so I made the rounds, "Hi kids; what's up?"

Ashley responded for herself and Jackie with a loud, "Sh!" and held her right index finger to her lips.

"Well thank goodness for educational programming," I said in a stage whisper and headed upstairs to have fun with the cash.

Before opening the trunk of the Chevy, I scanned the street and neighborhood for a police stakeout. `You might know; Harrington and his mangy hound. The stupid bastard's too friggin' nosey.' "Jesus, you are crazy!" I whispered before climbing to the carport storage area and hauling down the box of hundred dollar bills.

I carried the carton into the basement and drew up a folding chair to the utility table. From the original Lord & Taylor bag, I counted the bundles of hundred dollar bills. "Twenty."

Grabbing two bundles at random and without breaking the strap, I carefully fingered the bills and then counted them. "Fifty. Good old Matt, one of nature's noblemen; bastard!" After counting another wad of fifty, I exclaimed, "Good man!"

The second and third bags each contained eighteen strapped bundles of bills. Counting a bundle from each, I whispered, "Holy shit; two hundred and eighty thousand…Wow!" and emitted a very soft whistle of appreciation and whispered, "You're in the soup, Phelan, and you have to get this out of here."

Looking around the basement, I spotted a large flattened cardboard moving carton on the floor near the washing machine and hastily put it together by folding each of the bottom flaps over and under each other in turn. Placing the smaller box and the three shopping bags inside, I sealed it by interlocking the flaps on the top of the box. 'Easy; can't wake her; don't panic!' I thought.

Grabbing the box, I snuck back up into the kitchen and back out into the carport, trying very hard to appear normal. 'Not even close,' was my assessment.

Pushing the box as far back into the recesses of the storage space as possible, I thought, 'This is the dumbest hiding place in the history of man, but aside from the chest pains over the stupidity, it's probably better here, unlocked, than in a safe in the house. Nobody's ever burgled a carport storage area. Right?' Pressure in my chest increased to the point of real discomfort.

Trying to get back in presentable form before Jen saw me, I whispered, "Where can I really store it?"

Not having solved my problem despite some heavy thinking over the weekend, on Monday morning I saw Barrow walk into his office and quickly followed him in, closing the door behind me.

"What's up?" he asked.

"Another problem."

"Obviously."

"Where do you keep your money?"

"I'm supposed to tell you that?" After a purposeful pause he went on, "Oh, you mean generically," and added a chuckle.

"Yeah, generically. I've got an overflowing box of cash and don't know what the hell to do with it. You're the expert at everything; how do you deal with it?"

"You're rolling in dough and don't know where to turn. Not everybody in the world has to deal with such a pickle," Barrow said with obvious humorous disdain.

"Come on; cut the bull. I need your help."

"Getting the money's the easy part; making it useful to you is the real trick. We're all in the same bind. The IRS and Treasury are wise to the ways of we wicked wascals with warm cash," he said in a less than perfect attempt at alliteration in the voice of Elmer Fudd, "and laundering is a major cottage industry.

"Roby and Fred didn't consider it when they set this up, and it's plagued us ever since. I…"

"You got sucked in and you roped me in before you knew how to deal with this? You must have an attic full of hundred dollar bills… At least your heating bills must be low with all that insulation."

"I've said a lot of nasty things about Roby, but he's resourceful and smart on problems like this. He saw the problem and he's been working on it since day one. His end of it is pretty much under control with all those dummy corporations, the foundation, and the creative way he's got expenses coming out of his ears. You saw where he's headed with those real estate deals he's got simmering in Mexico. He's dropped hints that when those deals begin to materialize he'll be able to wash all of our laundry. From what I know of it, that will ease your heartburn big time."

"I'll be on Social Security before those deals help."

"Where you stash yours is up to you. But you better get with it before somebody finds it and blows up the whole shebang."

"Come on; what are you doing with yours?"

"I wish I could say, `enough', but it's not. I've tried every nickel and dime trick I could think of, but the only thing that works for me is to peel off a couple of bills every week and deposit them. I've only fallen behind by about fifty years so far," he said with an exasperated laugh.

"Remember I told you that I like nice things. Well, Amanda touted me on an art gallery in New York that specializes in up and coming artists; most of them are not at the very top level – but damn good. The gal who owns the place likes cash, and she's probably stiffing the painters. Every so often, maybe once every two or three months, I go up to Manhattan using planes, trains and automobiles and she has two or three paintings – of the right size – waiting for me. I hand over whatever she says in hundreds and head back home with them.

"She's got a good eye and a few of her choices have panned out well. I made a good profit on a couple of paintings by taking them to another gallery where she has a buddy and cashed them in; I mean I got checks for them – and reported the income. The wins pretty much offset the discounts I absorb on the losers. But it's a laundry that cleans fast and well – gets all the grit out. And they're very discreet, and I'll be glad to give the names of both galleries, but…"

"Don't bother; I could never pull that off. Jen would smell a rat in a second. Besides, I don't know anything about art, and with my paranoia, I'd be out of my mind no matter how I went to and from New York."

Barrow offered, "Self confessed Philistines have to find their own way. Give me points for trying to help."

I let the crap pass, and as I was just about to retreat to my office he opened up again, "Oh, I'm also an expert on gassing up my cars for cash. I use about a half a dozen gas stations and wait till I'm almost empty. Sometimes the clerks complain that they don't have enough change to deal with a hundred dollar bill, but I tell 'em I don't have anything else sufficient to cover the fill up and slip them a five or ten. I've found that tens will lubricate the transactions every time," he said with a snicker.

"I also volunteer to pick up groceries. I use quite a few stores, and…Oh, never offer your Giant or Safeway membership cards. You don't want any record on your accounts that confirm that you're paying with hundreds every week."

I saw an opening and said, "One way you could help is to push my promotion. Jen knows that we have to be close with our money. With a raise, I could squeeze in an extra hundred or two in the bank every payday. It isn't much, but it would ease some of my worst pain."

"I keep forgetting the differences in our lives. My wife's an elementary school principal in Prince William County and lets me handles the finances. No doubt it isn't as easy for you with the kids and Jen at home.

"My son's on his own, but I can slip him a hundred here and there without raising his suspicions. I don't suppose that tucking a Benjamin into your baby's diaper would work quite as well, but…"

"No it wouldn't, so?"

"I promised you the promotion and I'll make it happen, but I'm busy right now with actual Corps work. How about writing it up yourself? Do it for two grades; that way we won't have to post the job for everybody in the world the second year. Call Inez in Human Resources and tell her that we need it as soon as possible."

"You're doing well. You've been here what? Six years and you're being put in for a thirteen with another grade as a kicker."

I was annoyed. "Well none of the others have my real qualifications…partner."

"Right you are; nothing's too good for a partner."

I tried to diffuse the awkward situation, "I'll have the memo for you in ten minutes."

Barrow laughed, "Nothing like a little incentive to move things along. Approach your laundry and dry cleaning with the same attitude and all will be well."

EIGHTEEN

It was Jen on the phone, "I just finished talking with my mother. The forecast for the next few days looks really good, and she asked if I could drive up so my Dad could see the baby. I feel fine, but I was wondering if you might be able to get a few days off and go with me?"

"I'd like that, Love, but I'm swamped with the new job and all. Maybe I could drive you up on Saturday and come home on Sunday and do it again next week to pick you up."

"That's ridiculous. I'm fine. I can drive it easy."

"If you're really up to it that would probably be better. I'm sure my folks would lend me the Caprice while you're gone. That worked like a charm the weekend I was in Mexico and took our car to the airport. Mom's is big, but if you could handle it when you were huge, a big boy like me should be able to wrestle it around.

"Whatever, don't worry about me; I'll be fine. My folks have been hogging the kids…

"Hey, maybe my Mom could even use a break. I'll check with her right now about using the car; everything will work and you can stay as long as you want, even a week," I said hoping that sounded casual enough.

That Friday - with the door to my office closed – I watched the clock with more than normal interest. Thirty-two minutes after Jen's stated departure time I dialed her up, "Hey, it's me. How are you feeling?"

"For God's sake, Tommy, I'm not a damn invalid. I'm doing fine. It was a baby; I've had two others. Why are you bugging me? You know this isn't the easiest drive in the world."

"I just worry about you. Are the kids being good?"

"Jackie and the baby are sound asleep and Ash is being an angel.

"I couldn't be better, so just get off and let me drive."

Knowing her vocalizations like the back of my hand, there was no doubt in my mind that she was really annoyed. "Where are you?" I said, trying for just the right tone.

"I just got off the toll road and I'm passing by the last of the big Leesburg intersections on Route 15. I should be across the river and in Maryland in… maybe…ten…fifteen minutes.

"I'm fine, Tom. Now would you just let me drive? The road narrows to two lanes in a minute or so, and I really have to have two hands."

"Good girl. I was just concerned."

"Don't be." The phone went dead.

By the time I got home from work, my plan was fully formed – at least I thought it was. I raced to get the stash from the carport. Turning from the bottom of the step ladder to return to the kitchen, I spotted Harrington and his dog. `Keep your friggin' hound at your own end of the street, asshole. Could he be a money sniffing G-Dog?' I wondered and chuckled at my paranoia.

'Jesus, if I don't ease up, I'll wind up in the nut house. There has to be a `right' level of caution in this business, but, Tommy boy, you're at the fifth standard deviation over the top.'

The farther I got away from the carport and into the interior of the house where no one could see me, the better I felt. Placing the box on the basement work table, like a priest raising the Host, I lifted out the hundred thousand contained in the Lord & Taylor bag. "Now that is one pretty sight, Phelan; admit it. I do, I do," I said in the happiest conversation with myself I'd had in months.

Breaking the strap on a bundle of bills, I counted out five stacks of ten bills each. Carefully folding the stacks, I placed an oversize paper clip on each and lined them up like soldiers.

"Just to be safe," I said under my breath and broke open another bundle, doubling the size of my wad to ten thousand dollars.

Reaching the count of five on the first stack from the second bundle, I almost jumped through the door into the rec room when the damn doorbell went off like an air raid alert during the Blitz of London. Rising far too quickly, I dropped the rest of the bundle strewing bills across the table and watched a couple drift onto the concrete floor. "Shit!"

Racing up the stairs, I crossed the kitchen and caught a glimpse of my Dad's Civic parked out front. 'Lucky Mom didn't barge in like usual and come hunting for me,' I thought and reached to open the front door.

"Dad!" I said, shocked at greeting him.

"Yeah, Pat Phelan in the flesh; you expected maybe the King of England?"

"No...no...I...ah, ah... thought it was Mom. You...never... ah...almost never come over alone."

"My freakin' car staring you in the eyeballs and you expect your mother? Good luck with that. Hey, you're blocking the door; can I come in?"

"I'm sorry…oh, sure…come on in," I went into full stammer and, pointing to a chair, continued, "Sit down. What's up?"

"I ran an errand for Mom in Fairfax and thought I'd drop in on the way home to see how you're doing as a bachelor. I didn't mean to give you a heart attack. You OK? I mean you ain't got a broad in the closet have you? Got one for old Pat, I hope," he said with a hearty laugh

I tried to make my laugh sound genuine but knew that it was off the mark. "Funny man! I was just cleaning up in the basement and got pretty deep into it with nobody around to bug me."

"Yeah, well, how about taking a break and us having a brew? I let four o'clock pass to come by here, so it's like I'm in the Sahara. My tongue's cracking; you want me to croak right here?"

"I'm sorry; I was preoccupied." Instead of laughing, I was acting as if he meant his words.

As he rose, I realized that it was going to be a race to the basement refrigerator. `God!' I implored silently.

"Relax, I got 'em," he said.

Sitting between him and the kitchen, I jumped up in a panic and said, "No! No! I put some in the… the kitchen last night. We have to…ah… kill those first."

Almost running into the kitchen, I tore open the refrigerator and yelled back, "They're not here…she must have put them back downstairs before she left…I'm on it."

On my way through the basement, I flipped the open stash box under the table surface and swept the loose money and all of my carefully arranged stacks into it. Moving far too quickly, I gobbled up the bills from the floor and shoved the box onto the opposite side of the table well out of the path to the refrigerator.

Still racing, I grabbed two Budweisers and hustled up the stairs.

"What the hell's going on? You brewin' your own?"

My laugh sounded hollow even to my ears. "Sorry, I knocked over some junk and stopped to pick it up," I said, trying very hard to make my confession of ineptitude sound plausible. I twisted the top off one bottle like I was wringing a chicken's neck and handed it over; it's the old man's preferred method of drinking.

"Man, you are jumpy; take it easy.

"So, how's the new job going?"

Feeling the pain in my gut begin to subside, I relaxed and said, "It's really good. I've got a shot at a thirteen and maybe even a fourteen in a year or so."

"Wow, I was over fifty when I made my thirteen with the Navy...and that was it. You're living right. Everybody in the group's an accountant?"

"Mostly business and finance majors, but accountants, too... course all of 'em took accounting. And almost all of them are pretty sharp. The only guy without close to an accounting or finance background is the boss himself, a liberal arts man; he told me that he double majored in history and English. Then he went to law school but dropped out after a year; that's his claim to fame in the division and how he got into contracting."

"I know the type; can't tie their shoe laces or add up a column, but they're intellectuals who know everything, especially how to run the freakin' world."

"That's him...but he's easy enough to work for."

We went on and on about work and how being a fed had changed in the years since he retired.

"You're doing real good, Tommy; I'm proud of you. You got a nice wife and great kids. Mom and I think the world of Jen."

"I know, and I appreciate what I have, but sometimes I think I could do better outside of government."

"What? You just got through telling me what a damn hot shot you are – two grades almost in hand and already lapping your old man. Country's overrun with unemployed accountants, lawyers and engineers and you got steady work. What are you, freakin' nuts?"

"You're right; never mind," I said, sorry that I'd let my disaffection slip, but on the other hand, happy I'd set the stage for anything I might spring on him in the future.

I rose and walked to the bathroom. When got back, Dad was gone. Racing to the basement door, I yelled, "You down there?"

"Yeah, I'm getting a couple of more. I'll be right up."

I flew down the stairs and into the basement. 'A scene from a silent movie; if I wasn't out of my mind this would have been funny.' On the far side of the table, I saw two hundred dollar bills on the floor and almost had a heart attack. 'Lady Luck, don't forsake me now!'

I darted to a point between Dad and the strewn money, and as he bent over the beer lined up in the refrigerator door, as calmly as possible, I said, "Take the ones on the top shelf - not those in the door. They're older."

"OK; alright already; hey, don't get your ass in an uproar. God, you're as nervous as a stray cat in a dog pound. I really am going to check your closet for that broad."

I laughed and steered him out of the basement while trying to keep myself in the line of sight of the money.

I opened both beers, handed him one and plopped myself down again and thought, 'A home office for this partnership is not the way to go.'

We spent the next ten minutes talking baseball and killing the beer.

"Well, I got to go. Your mom will be thinking that we both have chicks over here."

"Yeah, right," I deadpanned.

The next morning I was ready and went to the mirror for one final check. My Orioles cap stood out. "No logos, moron! You're supposed to be invisible," I said under my breath.

Returning from the closet with a gray bucket style golf hat with no logo or other embellishment, I again checked my image, "Where'd she get this damn dog? A yard sale? Whatever; Woody Allen, total loser, perfect."

Placing my peanut butter sandwich and an apple on top of the napkins that were spread carefully over the stacks of hundred dollar bills in the bottom of the drab olive green lunch bucket, I still wasn't satisfied. 'This is the best you can do to look nondescript? Yes, best; fuck it.'

Minutes later, I pointed the Caprice toward Baltimore. "How long is a furlong?" I said with a laugh. I was on my way.

Mindlessly driving over the Potomac River into Maryland on the Woodrow Wilson Bridge, I fell in line with the traffic on the Capital Beltway through Prince George's County. Looking down I was horrified when I saw the speedometer reading seventy-five in a fifty-five mile an hour zone. Easing up, I pulled over into the right travel lane, and in another minute I was just as frightened to find myself doing the speed limit and having all the cars pass me like I was standing still…with a lot of them leaving digital salutes in their wakes.

I stayed in the right travel lane but pushed the car up to sixty-eight. The sounds coming from the engine and transmission reminded me that Mom rarely drove that fast, but I was unrelenting for the rest of the trip on the Beltway. This was the perfect nondescript speed that was most likely to get me to Pimlico without the need for a tete-a-tete with a Maryland State trooper, not the most sensitive conversationalists on the East Coast.

I was constantly distracted by trying to recall the points I thought were important that I'd highlighted on the guide for beginning bettors on the race track's website. `Twenty dollars across the board on number seven in the second race at Bay Meadows,' I practiced in my head. `Or is it sixty dollars with twenty each for win, place and show on seven…? It's OK, Phelan. All you have to do is sound normal… and confident; a bettor always expects to win.

'Remember, jackass, we ain't picking winners; we're doing our friggin' laundry. OK, so the favorite ten minutes before post time at whatever track is up next gets the bet, but only if the odds are less than two to one. Win or lose, we win forty bucks; anything the nag does is gravy.'

"You ready? You bet!" I shouted like an army drill sergeant and recruit foil in basic training.

Fortunately, when I turned onto the Baltimore Washington Parkway my troubles eased as my unfamiliarity with the road forced my attention away from my technical problems with horse racing and onto my driving.

The car seemed to sigh in relief when I shut it off in the Pimlico parking lot. I pulled out the copy I'd made of the 'Betting for Beginners' from the track website and began another review of my new system. 'Thank God I'm just laundering money and not trying to win. Havin' to make a buck would be way too much for the moron on this mission,' I thought, 'a jackass like me could lose some serious money with what I know.'

I pulled out five clips of hundred dollar bills and put them in my right front pocket. Tapping the lunch bucket and patting my front pocket, I was as ready as I was going to be and began the long walk across the parking lot to solvency and a new day.

I paid my way into the clubhouse with a twenty dollar bill and walked to the front railing. The weather was perfect, partly cloudy and in the mid seventies. I thought about the time when my Dad took me to Pimlico when I was about twelve. I remembered fondly the beauty of the track and its immediate surroundings, making sure that I didn't look too far past the grounds to some of the urbanized scenes beyond. `Race tracks are really nice,' I thought and tried to recall the huge crowd at the Preakness on that warm mid May afternoon so long ago.

There were few people in the clubhouse stands, and I moved back eight or ten rows and took a seat well away from members of the scant crowd. Repeatedly, I checked my front right pocket and convinced myself that I could pull out a single packet and not dump the rest and my story all over the floor.

Checking the program, I made ready for my first trip to the betting window. 'You're a player. A hundred dollar bill is nothing to you, right? Even if it isn't, you have to look like it isn't, right? You're not making any sense at all, right? Right! Just be cool; it will all work out.'

At ten minutes before post time for the first race, I checked the odds board and saw that the number three horse was a prohibitive favorite. Screwing up my courage I strolled to the betting window. "Sixty dollars across the board on number three in the first race here. That's twenty each on win, place and show. Right?"

"Right you are, sir," said the clerk placing my hundred in his box and punching out my ticket. "Good luck."

Picking another seat well back from the front, I downed my sandwich without the benefit of a drink. 'Why do I get the feeling that not too many clubhouse players are into dry peanut butter sandwiches?'

At almost the instant I was brushing the crumbs off of my hands, the gate flew open and my sixty bucks took off. The electricity in the air rose and the small crowd began to rumble and direct its attention to the track. As I followed the field, I realized that I had no clue on how my nag was doing. Fumbling with the program, I could not read and watch the race. 'Next race at least memorize the colors.'

As the horses entered the home stretch, the crowd began to scream for their horses, and it was clear that the three was the crowd's favorite – and mine too. As the race climaxed, I could read the numbers and saw that my horse was in a furious race with the number six. As they galloped across the finish line, there was little doubt that my dog had finished in second place by about a head. `Way to pick 'em!'

When the race was declared official, I found that I'd won sixty-four dollars. As I did my math, I could hardly contain my smile. My first hundred dollar bill and had netted me four dollars. "Now that's how you play the horses, Tommy Phelan," I said to an almost empty cavernous clubhouse.

As the afternoon progressed, my confidence rose even as my rate of return diminished. After using my inspired system on simulcast races at tracks on both coasts and half a dozen others in between, I made bets that used up every one of the bills I brought with me. In addition to the forty dollars change with every transaction, I guessed that my winning tickets now filling both of my front trouser pockets were pretty close to four thousand dollars. `You should have been a tout, not a memo writer, Tommy the Tout, Phelan!'

A major problem remained: how to collect my winnings. I didn't want them in cash. `This is one pot you want to pay your taxes on.' I scoured the material I'd downloaded from my computer and after rejecting mailing the dozens of winning tickets to the track, stumbled on my new method, the only obvious one.

After the last race at Pimlico, I took an empty seat in the nearly empty grandstand and put my winning tickets in order. Approaching a window without a line, I presented the package to the clerk and asked if he could have the proceeds in a check. The clerk whistled as he ran the tickets through his tote machine. "Wow! You've had a busy day, mister."

"Lot of luck," I replied, trying my damndest to look and sound casual.

A patron moved in behind me and the clerk said, "You might want to try another window, sir; this gentleman's transactions are going to take some time."

As I turned around, the man smiled and said, 'You hit the exacta?"

"No, but I lucked out on a few small ones."

A beautiful check for $4,210.40 in my wallet, I headed for the parking lot doing my best to blow through, 'I Whistle a Happy Tune.' Settling myself in Mom's Chevy, I said, "Not bad for a guy who doesn't remember the tune and can't get a note out on half the blows...And I'm not afraid... well, not too afraid."

"OK now how do I tell Jen about Tommy's big day at the track? More fucking lies…deeper gets the hole."

I grabbed a beer and sat at the work table to verify my losing tickets. "Not bad. Not many losers when you bet heavy favorites across the board. So you're down…what? …A couple of thou. You made yourself more than seven grand today, smart boy. Not everybody makes out by losing; right? Makes no sense…big deal." I figured that I'd have to pay taxes on almost none of it. "Just another day at Phelan's Chinese Laundry, open under new management."

Suddenly, it struck me; this would never work. In almost nothing flat, I would be leaving a paper trail a mile wide and ten miles long. Depressed, I waltzed into the basement and grabbed another brew. "At least you'll have a fist full of cash from today… We'll always have Paris!"

'Let's see,' 'Well you see, Jen, one of the guys at the office was going to Pimlico, and when he found out I was home alone, he invited me to go with him. By shit luck, I won a couple of races, and since I was playing with house money, I took a flyer on the pick six. Damned if I didn't hit it for four grand.'

"Not a chance in the world!" I said aloud.

"Lucky boy, you're the keeper of the money in the house. Just put it in the bank and don't say a word. How many lies can you tell and how many felonies can you compound, Thomas?

"You, Phelan, are working on your own entry in the Guinness Book of World Records."

NINETEEN

"Got a minute?" was John Barrow's greeting when I entered the outer office.

Since this was rarely a sign of good news, I went right to `battle stations' as he closed his door behind him. "What's up?"

"Nothing, except that you are now officially my new special assistant, fully upgraded and in line for another promotion in a year without any need for more paperwork. Congratulations!"

"Wow! That's great, John. Thanks for everything," I said as my blood pressure slowly backed out of the red zone.

"I don't know if you'll believe this, but I couldn't have made a better choice under any and all circumstances. I'm sorry that you were roped into... but you really are good at what you're doing and I look forward to having you next door."

"That really does make me feel good. I know you were under a lot of pressure and I know that what happened to me wasn't your call. Actually, I like the work. It's a lot better than what I was doing, to say nothing about the extra income. And what flexibility it will afford me in dealing with my `other' situation."

"Well enough of this love in. You're the man, and you deserve it. Now get to work."

"You bet."

Almost trotting into my office, I dialed Jen. "I got the promotion! We can buy a car."

The relief in her voice was evident, "Oh, Tommy, that's really great. And you were right; a car for you should be our number one priority. Three kids, shopping, pediatricians – it's swamping me…us.

"That's the best news in months. I'm so proud of you. I told you that you had a future with the government."

"I know. Hey scrub dinner; we're going out to Angie's for the biggest Greek salads and pizzas that money can buy."

When we got home from our big evening out and feeling full of myself, I settled down to check all the car ads in the Post. It took only a couple of minutes to come up with what I thought was the most promising phone number and I punched it in, "Hello, my name's Tom Phelan. I'm calling about the Toyota Camry you advertised. Have you sold it?"

The response was negative.

"Could I come by and look at it?"

"Great. Where do you live?"

"That's only three or four miles from my house. Can I come over now?"

It only took me ten minutes in the dingmobile, and as I stepped out of the car I was met out front of the neat split level by the owner, Howard Peterson.

"She's clean as a whistle with nothing wrong. It's got 42,000 miles and could use new tires. That's it…and maybe a new battery."

"You're ad said $8,900. That's firm?"

"As the Rock of Gibraltar."

"What are you replacing it with?"

"That's it right there," Peterson said, pointing to a shiny new Camry lodged in the carport behind him. "Had good luck with this one and wasn't about to change.

"Look, Mr. Phelan, I've never sold a car privately before, and I hate to be a pain, but this whole thing is beyond me. If you don't mind, I'm going to have to have a cashier's check, if you buy it."

My heart leaped; I was about to make Howard's day, "I know how you feel. If I were in your spot, I'd be just as concerned.

"Tell you what; if you'd be more comfortable, maybe I could work it out to pay you in cash. It would take another day or two for me to get it from my bank, but if you'd feel better about it, I'd be glad to do it."

"That would be better, lots better. I appreciate it....That would be great."

"How about we take her for a spin?"

The next Monday morning, John greeted me, "Good morning, Tom. Have a good weekend? "

"I've got me a new set of wheels. Took your advice and paid cash for a used Camry in a private sale.

"Almost killed the guy I bought it from by not trying knock the price down and then by saying I'd give him cash. I thought he was going to flop right there with a massive coronary. When I left after the test drive, I looked in my mirror and saw him run – I mean run – into the house to tell his wife he had just made the score of his life."

Barrow had a rapturous laugh – interrupted by some heavy hacking. "I've caused that reaction a couple of times; it's awesome, eh? The power of Benjamin Franklin inspires awe in me even two centuries after his demise."

TWENTY

Jenifer was off to a Saturday lunch and a baby shower for one of her friends, and she was going to drop off the kids with my folks on her way. I expected her to be gone for hours and the plan for the day was to deal with the growing stash of cash in the carport. 'Thank God for moms,' I thought. At eleven-thirty, the stated arrival time for the lunch, I hauled down the box from the storage space and tossed it in the trunk of the Camry and headed for the Pentagon City Mall. I drove to the third level of the garage and moved as far from the mall entrance as possible before parking.

A man on a mission, I walked boldly through the mall and into a luggage store and quickly selected and bought a large aluminum travel case. Hey, what did you expect; this is Tommy Phelan's treasure not rations for rodents. Returning to the car and with only a casual visual sweep of the area, I opened the trunk, inserted the new case and transferred all of the money from the cardboard box into it.

With another quick look around, I marched back into the mall with my luggage in tow and took the escalator down into the Metro station and boarded the next train bound for Reagan National Airport. 'Tommy, either you're getting braver or even more stupid. Which is it?' I smiled as I approached the Enterprise car rental counter in the airport.

"Hi, my wife called and won't be able to pick me up. Is there any chance you have an available car?"

There was indeed such a vehicle at the ready and I was quickly on my way to the rental storage facility on Lee Highway just past Shirley Gate Road beyond Fairfax City. Negotiating for one of the smallest units and paying in cash for a year in advance, all under the name of Howard Kurtz, one of my favorite yet obscure TV personalities, at a street address that I knew did not exist. I quickly made my deposit, locked the roll top door, and reversed course to the airport where I casually explained to the return clerk that my car problems had been solved and took a train back to Pentagon City and drove home in time to be casually sipping a beer when Jen arrived with the children in tow. "You are improving, Phelan," I complimented myself as I heard the doors to the Chevy slam shut.

"Hi, everybody! Did everybody have a nice day?"

The two older children raised their voices in uniform shout of, "Yes!" and Ash added, "Grampa took us for a pony ride."

"What a nice Grampa," I said.

TWENTY ONE

As the months passed, in the face of my new routine of government existence, even a thoroughly paranoid individual like me couldn't help but lower his guard as the drops at the storage center became routine. Still, I was careful to use a different rental car company with each visit to the facility and to wear my most ordinary and benign costumes, but I still smiled to the uniformed employees at the guard station and confidently made my deposits into an increasing number of metal travel bags. I also became aware that aluminum mining in this unit might be profitable when the great Alaska charity was shut down.

My confidence in passing hundred dollar bills also increased as the seasons changed. While I was rapidly falling behind the ever expanding treasure in the storage unit, at least I was able to pass a sufficient number of bills which coupled with my expected promotion was already permitting a slight upgrade in the Phelan family standard of living without causing Jen or my folks to suspect anything out of the ordinary.

So it was that when John Barrow walked into my office and closed the door, I was no longer automatically on high alert.

"Mornin', John. What's up?"

Without being asked, he pulled up a chair and sat close to my desk. "I've got some less than great news for the company," he said, and without waiting for the usual banter, "You remember I was out sick last Monday?"

"Yeah."

"I got the word Friday afternoon that I have lung cancer."

On full alert and in a state of high anxiety, I almost shouted, "God damn it, John; those friggin' weeds. I told you…"

"It doesn't matter what you and Evelyn and everyone else told me. It is what it is. I'm scheduled for surgery next Tuesday at Fairfax Hospital.

"I'll be out of the office for about a month, so get all of the Alaskan invoices you need to have signed on my desk today."

I watched as Barrow aged right in front of my eyes and thought, 'God, I'm going to wind up in deep shit all by my lonesome.'

Barrow went on, "I'll call Roby and tell him that everything has to be finished by Monday, and…"

"No, you take it easy; I'll call and let him know what's up."

"Thanks, I appreciate it."

He left and I closed the door. Pulling out my wallet on my way back to the desk, I found the slip of paper with a single four digit number on it, and after entering the known six digit prefix, I dialed the numbers in reverse order.

"Yeah?" the surly voice responded.

"You a praying man?"

"Cut the crap. Let's have it."

"Our main man in Belvoir is going to undergo lung cancer surgery next Tuesday at Fairfax Hospital."

"What?" was the startled response.

"You heard right. If he croaks on the table, you and I will soon be bunkies at the Gray Bar Motel."

"How bad is it?"

"He didn't say, but he looks to be about a thousand – maybe fifteen hundred - years old."

"OK, keep me posted; oh, and don't be such a jackass about it."

I settled down long enough to smile at Roby's obvious discomfort but unfortunately had to return to the moment and face my own worst fears. 'Holy shit, this could be it!'

I spent the rest of the week and the weekend in quiet isolation, panic just below the surface. Shortly after lunch on Tuesday, Pearl came to the door. "Mrs. Barrow just called. Everything went well. John's in recovery and resting comfortably."

"That's great, Pearl. I appreciate it; keep me posted," I said trying to control the appearance of my overwhelming relief.

"Oh, this just came up from HR for you," she said handing me an envelope. "If I'm not mistaken it's the official notice of your promotion."

As Pearl hovered, I tore open the package and pulled out the forms. "You nailed it."

"Congratulations; it's a pleasure to work with you, Tom. John said that you'd be a great addition and was he ever right."

"That's very kind of you, Pearl; I think that you're super, too."

After she left, I dug for my wallet but didn't pull out the paper I'd been seeking. 'Bullshit, you're going to have to call me, asshole. You won't know shit unless you ask.'

Shortly after three o'clock my phone rang as I was sitting alone in the cafeteria with a cup of coffee. I checked the incoming and smiled, 'My man.'

"Hello," I said blandly.

"Have you heard anything?"

"He came through it like a champ and is resting comfortably."

"Thanks for sharing," Roby said and hung up.

That Thursday evening, I drove over to the hospital and after some difficulty in solving the extraordinary maze that is the regularly added to, amended and always under construction hospital, found myself at the door of John Barrow's room. I was pleased to see that he was wide awake and smiling at me. The only other person in the room was his wife whom I remembered from Fred Callahan's wake.

"Tom, how nice of you to come," Barrow whispered hoarsely. "You've met Evelyn?"

"I'm glad you're looking so well and alert, John. Nice to see you again, Mrs. Barrow."

"Thank you for coming, Tom. Please call me Evelyn. Doesn't he look good? It was a long and difficult surgery, but he came through like a man twenty years younger."

"Evelyn, you remember meeting Tom at Fred Callahan's wake. He was directly behind us in the receiving line."

Mrs. Barrow smiled warmly, "Of course.

"John's told me a lot about you, Tom. I'm so pleased that he's awake; he's been sleeping through most his other guests' visits; he's definitely on the mend and will be back at the office in just a matter of weeks. Isn't that right?"

"Not a doubt in the world," was the raspy whispered reply before his eyes fluttered.

Already feeling that I'd overstayed my visit, I made some small talk about all the beautiful flowers sent by relatives and friends and about the fine weather. It was apparently soothing balm and Barrow soon drifted off to sleep, and I made as polite an exit as I could muster.

Harold Mortenson, the dams and levees branch chief, was designated to serve as division director in Barrow's absence. Harold would remain in his office on the second floor, so Pearl and I were left in isolation to shuffle the papers needed to keep the shop running with several mail runs to Mortenson's office each morning and afternoon.

Three weeks after the operation, John phoned me, "I'm going to be out longer than expected. It will be at least six weeks total before my doctor clears me to return to work."

"Nothing too serious, I hope."

"Oh no; but despite the rosy baloney the surgeon gave Evelyn and me in recovery, I just wasn't in as good shape as most patients when I was operated on and I'm somewhat slower in bouncing back. But everything's fine.

"I called Harold, and he has no problem continuing as acting. He said that you were doing fine upstairs.

"I'm feeling better every day, but I'm a little tired now, so I'm going to sign off and take a little nap. I'll see you in a few weeks."

Weeks later, I was at my desk at around eight o'clock and was drinking my first cup of coffee when I saw John enter the outer office. He was using a cane and was walking with tiny, slow steps, stopping to rest every few feet. I rose and watched Pearl race to embrace and assist him into his office. 'Dead as a fucking door nail.' was my judgment as I rose to follow him.

John settled into his chair with a final plop as he didn't have the strength to support and lower his body gradually. I turned and read Pearl's face as she hovered over John and was convinced that she felt the same way.

"Would you like coffee, John?"

"That would be nice, Pearl. Thank you," he replied in a voice hardly above a whisper.

On her way out, she raised her eyes and gave a look that to me was a clear sign of despair.

I entered and with as cheery a smile as I could muster said, "Welcome back, John."

"Thanks. After Pearl brings the coffee, there are things that have to be done."

When Pearl entered we were smiling and discussing the draft choices that the Redskins might make.

I followed her to the door and closed it.

"Last Wednesday, my doctor gave me the word. He didn't get it all…couldn't, and I began a regimen of radiation and more chemicals than Dow produces.

"I haven't yet told Evelyn, but he said that I probably have somewhere between six months and a year."

"I'm sorry," I said as sincerely as possible – and as I truly felt.

"Thanks; I know, and while I'm frightened, there are no real alternatives. This was always my plan, but now it seems that maybe I should have considered my options somewhat more carefully before taking up smoking again."

"You started smoking to commit suicide?" I was incredulous.

"Not very conventional, eh? I've read about the reactions of the few guys who survived their swan dives from the Golden Gate Bridge. They all said that the instant they jumped, they regretted their actions. My regrets don't go that far back – only to the visit to my surgeon's office the day he gave me the word.

"I was ashamed and full of guilt over caving to Roby and Fred. Not only am I afraid of guns and hanging and whatever other means of achieving my goal, I figured that a hole in the head would bring down the enterprise and might draw Evelyn and my son, Fred, into it."

"John, that was ridiculous thinking."

"You think?" he said with a weak chuckle. "Well it's done. Actually I've lasted a lot longer than I figured and was able to launder a goodly share of my...ah...winnings. You and Fred with your numbers and columns and debits and credits may have had the score figured to the dime, but despite all my sloppiness and poor record keeping, I did quite well in doing my laundry.

"It sounds old fashioned, but I paid off my thirty year mortgage in just over five years, and without me to go to trial, they'll play hell trying to undo that.

"I've also got a bunch of paintings in storage – in Evelyn's name – that may not pay off at a hundred cents to the dollar but will still be worth a good deal some day."

"Why are you telling me all this?"

"I still have a lot of dirty hundreds, and you're the only person who can help me."

"What?"

"I'm going to give all of it to you. I want you to keep an eye out for my Fred. If he gets in financial difficulty, you can slip him a little something occasionally. If not, it's yours to try to get into your own income stream."

"I can't possibly guarantee anything like that. I could die before he does. If he needs a load of dough, I could never get away with giving it to him without exposing myself as a crook. Even if I were half as loyal as you seem to think, I can't assume responsibility for your family."

"I know all that, but I trust you to do what you can under the circumstances, using your own good judgment. The odds are infinitely better than just leaving it for the feds to find."

"Why not give it to Fred outright?"

"It won't work. I'd just turn him into a felon and it would be confiscated before it was of any use. You're already caught up in the mess, so there's no harm.

"Did I ever tell you that we named Fred after Callahan?"

"Bet you'd like to reconsider that one," I said coldly, but when I saw John sag even further, I said, "I mean the name, not Fred himself," and added a hollow laugh signifying – poorly – that it was intended as a joke.

John formed a wan smile and I continued, "Whatever, I'm not swearing to anything. Besides, if you really do die before this all crashes, all of your federal benefits and what you've done to set Evelyn up are bound to take care of her and Fred better than anything I could ever do. Do you have insurance?"

"Do I have insurance? Oh, yeah, in spades; let me tell you about my insurances: life, long term care, you name it; that's one of the big benefits of being in the laundry business.

"I forgot to mention that to you; you ought to take care of that for your wife, too," he said in an aside.

"Damn, John, Evelyn and Fred are going to have ten times more than they'll ever need as it is."

"Just do what you can. I think there's between three and four hundred thousand in the storage unit I rent in Manassas, and there'll be a few more invoices due before the current contract is complete. So what are we talking about? Maybe another hundred and fifty and maybe something north of half a million in total.

"By the way, push Roby hard on getting those invoices in," he demanded with a slightly stronger voice.

He then went back to the hidden money, "My cash in storage is a handy hunk of change that I don't ever want to undermine what Evelyn has."

"Shit, John, this stink pot could come down on us tomorrow. How the hell can I – or anyone - promise eternal devotion to crap like this? If you're planning on me to repeal the rules of lack of honor among thieves, you've got the wrong guy."

"No, I've got not only the right guy but the only one. All I'm asking is that you do your best. That's it. I'm done for, and it's the best I can do under the circumstances. Not a soul other than you knows anything about this…and my personal situation. Evelyn knows nothing; Fred knows nothing…And I don't intend to tell them anything. As I said so long ago, `…it borders on perfect.' Just do what you can."

"I'm not taking any ridiculous risks; I swear it," I said defiantly.

"I'm not asking you to. I'll let you know when I have the money and we'll work out how to exchange it."

Later that day, I took a break to the parking lot and called Roby, "We have to meet right away."

"Can you make it to Union Station tomorrow at two o'clock? The Center Café in the Main Hall…just sit at one of the tables out front."

"I'll be there before you."

The next afternoon, I watched as Matt casually sauntered up to a table in front of the café in the Main Hall of the great rail station on Capitol Hill. With no obvious preparatory security screening, Roby sat. "So what's this so very important meeting about?"

"The end of our partnership; Barrow's dying, and we've got just a few months the sweep it up and put it to bed."

The color in Roby's face went to chalk before my eyes. "Bullshit, you're being ridiculous, hysterical as always. We can get somebody else… I can rig it for you to become the division director. We can…"

"None of that is going to happen. I'm resigning from this outfit…done, through. I'm not going to cooperate any more. You've made millions. I've made a bundle, more than I can ever hope to convert into real money. This is our chance to put this to bed and maybe even get away with it."

Matt spoke softly but with great determination, "Listen up, I've still got you by the short hairs, and…"

I was ready for that one. "Knock that shit off! All your god damn leverage over me is gone. You can't share a fucking thing about me with anybody without blowing yourself up in the process, so get real. We can put this thing to sleep and pray that we get away with it, or we can try to patch it up and almost certainly expose ourselves to the FBI.

"Matt, it's time. Let's put it to bed and hope that we never see each other again."

Roby sat dumbly, obviously stunned.

After a moment, I went on, "The odds will never be this good again. My personal situation is OK. It's going to take me twenty years to convert the dough I have already, and in the meantime, I've got more than enough to get by.

"You've been working for years to launder your share and create all those phony fronts. It's time. We've got to do it. We're going to do it; right?"

Still Roby said nothing.

"We have to quit cold turkey, Matt. If we do, we might survive; if not, we don't have a chance. So, you're OK with it, right?"

After not speaking for perhaps another minute and with the silence now heavy, he said softly, "You may be right, but it's not going to be easy."

"I'll take that as full agreement," I said with force. "Get those last invoices to me as soon as you can and pray that John can get back to work and sign off on them before he croaks.

"I'm sure this will break your heart, but we should never be in contact again. Tell Amanda I said, `Goodbye'."

I thought that it looked like a race to see who could leave first. 'I won,' I thought as we hurried away. I turned in time to see him disappear. "Fuck you," I whispered and flipped him a hidden bird.

TWENTY TWO

Tumbling, somersaulting and yawing uncontrollably into a black abyss, I grasped madly for the small branches of the stunted scrub oaks growing from the cliff wall that I passed at ever accelerating speed. Screaming but emitting no sound, finally I saw the giant boulders rising to meet me at warp speed and onto which I would inevitably crash and splatter like a bug. Slamming into a large flat rock, I was badly shaken but unhurt and wide awake. 'I will be caught; I will be shamed; I will be convicted; I will go to prison; I will lose Jen; I will lose my kids; I will be ruined. There's no way out. I've been a fool from the beginning,'

My mind was perfectly clear; all my rationalizations were laid bare before me. All scenarios led to that same boulder; the enterprise was doomed – and I was a key player on the team.

"Tommy, wake up, wake up! You're having a terrible nightmare. Wake up!"

Aware of my situation almost immediately, I responded rationally, "I'm awake, Babe, wide awake. It was just a dream. I'm OK now," I said, stoically accepting my fate.

"You're soaked through; I've never seen you in such a state. Relax, Tommy. I'm here for you; everything's alright," she said embracing me tightly.

"I'm fine, Jen." By this point, I was sitting up ramrod straight, the blankets and linen were tossed and tangled everywhere.

She said, "Easy, baby; I can put everything back the way it was."

'If only,' I thought while jumping out of bed and heading for the bathroom. It was ridiculous from the beginning. The day Callahan and Barrows signed off on the first invoice, it was doomed, and I was stupid enough to join. How could it not have been clear to me from the outset?

If Callahan could spot the hole in the system, so could – and would - any number of disgruntled and larcenous employees across the entire federal candy store, and one day – sooner rather than later - the FBI would tell Tommy Phelan to assume the position against the wall.

Roby was right; I had rationalized my way in because I thought that I had a way out, but it's clear, I'm doomed.

Entrapped! Blackmailed! Physically threatened! Yeah, right; good luck selling those.

The ceiling light and all the lamps were blazing as Jen wrestled with the strewn sheets and blankets. I grabbed my pillow and headed for the stairs and the rec room couch.

"Tommy, don't go. Come back to bed. Everything will be OK"

"I'm wide awake. I can't sleep. I'll just keep you awake."

"That's OK, I don't care. You need your rest. You'll sleep."

"I'm not coming back. I'll do better on the couch. I'm going down."

Laying on the couch under the quilt we shared to watch TV, I was desperate as the scenarios scrolled before my eyes. 'Callahan and Barrow found their escape routes. A Metro train stamping a nice logo on my chest would do, but Tommy Phelan is definitely not one preferring death to dishonor. No sir, Tommy's afraid of the dark, doubly so now that I know what's out there waiting for me.'

"Come on, bright boy, you've got till dawn," I whispered.

Countries that do not have extradition treaties with the United States seemed the only solution. Naturally I didn't have a clue about which ones they were but simply assumed that all of the unpleasant lands that I could think of were on the list, and each time one entered my consciousness, it was rejected on familial, lingual, cultural or climatologic grounds.

'Tommy, boy, you are slated for a room for two with a tattooed biker named Big John as your roommate, so unless you want to commit bigamy with a weightlifter, you're going to have to dig deeper.'

Despite the adrenaline rush from the nightmare that caused my mind to race madly, I found myself drifting off to sleep when suddenly epiphany in hand, I bolted upright wide awake and in possession of my Eldorado. It wasn't as neat and tidy – or final - as those used by my leaders, but it had a lot more panache, and the lack of actual pain and the chance that I wouldn't have to write new wedding vows made it possible for me to smile. "I'll just give the money back, every damn dime. And I'll sing like the biggest and brightest screaming yellow canary in the world, the Elvis of song birds. Bring on the lights!"

Before there was a hint of light at the point of day, I scampered up the stairs and into bed with my sleeping love and quickly fell into a deep sleep.

Two days later, I watched as Barrow pulled into the parking space beside mine in the far reaches of the Shoppes of Lorton Valley lot on Route 123. John struggled to get out of his car and had great difficulty in opening the trunk. 'Man, how much longer?' I thought.

Making no effort to appear innocent while transferring the two large cardboard boxes into my car and without even checking to see if they contained currency, I turned to him and snapped, "No promises - not a single one!" with barely restrained anger.

John replied, "None expected; just let your conscience be your guide."

"Hear me; I have no god damn conscience; it died when I joined the gang," I said vehemently.

Barrow said nothing else and wrestled his way back into his car and slowly pulled out onto the highway and headed north. I waited several minutes before driving in the opposite direction into the town of Occoquan. Finding a parking spot on Poplar St., I began a five minute window shopping tour of the shops while casually checking for anyone making the similarly timed stops.

Leaving the town I headed north on the interstate and made the extra long loop to my storage shed in Fairfax by way of the Beltway and Route 50. Making the first trip into the facility in my own Toyota and making no effort to cover my tracks, I smiled while greeting the guards and talking my way into the grounds.

"Damn good thing some people are organized," I said softly while opening my unit. Removing the boxes from my trunk, I moved them into the shade of the unit. Working feverishly, I transferred one hundred and seven thousand dollars into one of the aluminum cases. Breaking the paper wrap on perhaps a dozen bundles of bills and rewrapped them with heavy rubber bands.

I then placed the manila envelope containing the incriminating evidence that Barrow had stabbed me with as the ordeal began. I laughed when recollecting his smart assed remark about Juanita finding me attractive. "Now that was funny, you son of a bitch," I said laughing so hard that I coughed uncontrollably, reminding me of Barrow.

Back to my task, I placed four additional bundles of fifty hundreds wrapped in rubber bands and twenty loose bills in a letter size envelope inside a still larger Magruder's brown paper shopping bag.

On the way out of the facility, I casually strolled into the office and paid cash for two additional years in advance.

Burning up a month's worth of gas, I continued my great circle by driving south on Route 123 once again to another storage facility that I knew just north of Lorton and boldly rented another unit under still one more assumed name and transferred what remained of John Barrow's stash. I didn't have time to count it but gave it a quick eyeballing. "Has to be more than a quarter of a mil," I whispered, "Well, at least it's a plan."

Over the next two months, the last two invoices on the final contract from Roby landed on my desk. Barrow struggled into the office and did his final good deeds for the team and the papers proceeded to finance for payment and – I surmised – wafted their way to the great salt mine for centuries of extra slow composting.

One afternoon when John seemed particularly robust – for a dying man, he walked slowly into my office and sat for what was clearly going to be one of his philosophical performances.

"Coffee's coming; there are some more things we have to go over before I'm unable to deal with them."

He rested and we were silent as we waited for Pearl.

Within minutes she arrived with the goods. "While I've offered a few times, this is the first time John asked me to get coffee in what has to be more than ten years. You must need a caffeine jolt pretty badly," she said smiling.

"I do Pearl, I do. Thank you so much," he replied. We watched her leave and close the door behind her.

He turned to me and began speaking as if he were on a mission, "Obviously I'm not going to be able to help you much longer. It's clear now – if it ever wasn't – that I'm never going to get to the other world I've been describing for you, but I know you can get to it if you make it your most important goal. I only wish I could have lasted a couple of more years to really boost you along.

"It's a society of wealth and privilege that's yours for the taking. The funny thing is that it's populated by human beings just like us except for one thing: they're the capitalists. Like I told you, we're not; we're just workers. We could be communist workers or feudal workers. Workers are workers. Communists bullshit themselves that there's no difference between the bosses and the workers but everybody knows better. In feudal systems there wasn't a chance of becoming the lord of the manor if you weren't born to it. But in this capitalist world anyone with gumption, talent and a bit of luck can make it."

"John, don't feel like you have to kill yourself right here. You know I've got a pretty good handle on your thinking, so don't sap your strength. You…"

"Hear me out!" he interrupted.

"Don't worry about not being accepted if you can figure a way across the divide. Like us, capitalists have all the ordinary human frailties. They're weak or strong; venal or trustworthy; and have all the other good and bad characteristics of those of us in the world of wage slaves, but they – or their rich uncles - broke the code, so instead of just living in America, they own and run it and take the lion's share of the benefits," he said and rested to cough and regain his strength.

"Let it go, John. You don't have to convince me. You need to go home and rest."

"No; there are things I didn't say clearly enough. You think that you're cheating your way into that crowd, but they don't give a damn; in is in. You think the founders of all of the great families got there because they acted like Mother Teresa? Aside from guys like Bill Gates and Steve Jobs and that kind who got there by really creating things, a lot of them got there by legally bilking their fellow man, and more than a few by out and out swindling them. Trust me; you won't be alone in having to weasel word your way into heaven."

I smiled, "I've been practicing my speech for St. Peter, but since I'm an out and out thief, it gets a little dicey," I said with a laugh.

John chuckled but continued, "I don't know anything about the Pearly Gates, but the big boys and girls don't give a damn if you're imperfect or how you got there, only how you behave when you're in. They're just human beings who broke the code and had the guts to act on it. Like every other group, they divide up into blacks and whites – and confused grays, Democrats and Republicans – and confused independents, and they fight among themselves as badly as any bunch of workers, maybe more. There's never been a human institution or society that didn't ultimately divide into lefts and rights, with the in-betweens shifting the balance of power between the first two.

"But one thing's certain, they're the capitalists, and they know it. That's the club, but as soon as they arrive, they pick a side – or not: There's the loud mouth liberty type screaming their Ayn Rand bullshit who race to the right side of the room.

"Then there's the left which like the right divides its own three ways between those who are motivated – at least a little - by something akin to the Golden Rule and would help the downtrodden to some degree – at least with the right's tax money, if not their own, and those who aren't liberal but who never got past their fear of the French Revolution and are afraid of the mob and want to buy them off, and then there's the rest – maybe most of them - who quietly go about selling the burgers in their ten fast food franchises or tires in the their small chain of stores or running their hedge funds or whatever.

"So it doesn't really matter whether Atlas shrugs, flinches or just cringes, they're in and everybody else - no matter how smart just has or needs a job."

"That's a pretty cold and calculating analysis; I'll keep it in mind as I develop my lesson plan for my prison seminar on making it big on the outside," I said with an admiring smile.

But he appeared obsessed and went on as if he hadn't even heard me, "There are many, many trials in front of you, Tom, and I don't envy you the trip. But I saw early on that you were the partner who could bring us through the rapids. But Callahan and I won't be with you, and, of course, Roby is blind to that side of you and can't successfully make it without you," he said, and rested again for a moment, "You have to see clearly where you are going and avoid the many traps that will be laid along the way.

"You know, of course, that Roby can't stop. He'll go full speed ahead until he ruins everything, so you'll have to find a way to survive that calamity."

"I know you're right about that," I said. "And I know now that the scheme wasn't even close to perfect. It took me a long time to see that it was doomed the minute that you guys took the first step. Obviously, if Fred could break it, others can, and sooner or later someone will get busted. With that first break, the FBI hounds will be on our trails instantly and those beautifully preserved invoices in the salt mine will be just as fresh and clean as the day they were sent to decay over ten thousand years."

"The day that popped into my head was the day I started smoking again."

"You knew that when you did me in?" I said brusquely.

"Don't be angry, Tom, please. I came to see that it would go down, but I thought that if we could talk Roby into shutting down when we had enough that we might all be dead before they caught us. Obviously, that was a foolish thought; there's never enough for Roby. Besides, you know that I was trapped into the scheme, and, by now, you have to know that I'm really quite a weak character.

"But I've come to believe that you're the partner who can pull off the Houdini escape and magically get to the other side."

"John, I know that you're very sick and in spite of that, I have to say this: you don't know shit! I've spent countless hours, sleepless nights, thinking of ways to escape this stupid web that you fools – we fools – created. Obviously, this isn't going to end well for any of us. So go home while you have the strength and…"

He coughed but fought to interrupt me, "No, damn it; you can pull it off, Tom, you can. You can make it out of this maze and thrive and prosper."

Finally spent, he simply stopped chattering. He even had difficulty finishing his coffee. When he did, without asking, I walked around my desk and helped him up and walked him back into his office.

At the end of the day, I gave him my arm and walked him to his car. "You sure you can handle this?"

"I'm fine. The car knows its way home," he said with a chuckle as I helped him in.

I watched with anxiety, but the car pulled away in a fashion that gave me hope that he'd make it.

Over the coming weeks, the money drops were made and John had just enough strength to rendezvous with me in the Lorton shopping center and hand over his shares to me. I made my last two trips to the Fairfax storage facility and deposited my cut along with an updated balance sheet showing that every penny that I had ever acquired from Roby – directly - had been loaded into these aluminum valises. I also added to the contents of the paper bag with the proceeds from all minor transactions over the years. Every dime was documented and ready for collection and audit by the FBI. "They made me do it," I said while driving away. "It's the best I can do," I added as my mood sunk.

Shocking me, John's health seemed to improve and I wondered if the surgeon's assessment might have missed the mark. By mutual agreement, there was no more talk of Roby, Callahan or anything else connected with their withdrawals from the First National Bank of Ft. Belvoir.

After about six months, I doubted my appraisal of the end game for the company, but after every beer hoisted in joy, two representing reality followed and sent me into the now recurring deep dark depression that Jen could no longer relieve.

TWENTY THREE

"Tommy, I have to talk with you. I gotta come over right now," Jimmy Frawley whined in what I interpreted to be an all out panic mode.

"No, `How's your ass?' No, 'I'm gonna kick your useless butt at golf!' Is it really that bad?"

"Yeah... No; worse!"

"Give me twenty minutes to help with the cleanup after dinner. Then you're good to come over."

By the time he arrived, Jen and the kids had cleared out of the kitchen and were down in the rec room watching TV.

It was obvious that Jimmy had been bending his elbow for hours. "What the hell's up, man?"

Almost falling into the proffered seat at the table, Jimmy said in a slightly slurred manner, "You know what you told me was stupid to do? Well I did it."

"What the hell are you talking about? Slow down; speak English."

"That rental project over in Fairfax that you said was ridiculous; that I would be giving a third mortgage on that would blow up in my face if I bought it. I bought it for zip down. I gave a third for two hundred thousand bucks, assumed a second for another hundred and fifty, and the first for almost one point two million."

"And?"

"I can't make the payments. The rents barely cover the first mortgage, and... and like you said, the bubble blew up in my stupid fuckin' face. I'm into my old man for almost twenty grand, and the guy I bought it from has taken up residence in my driveway, screaming and weeping like a maniac for his dough.

"I'm completely tapped out, Tommy... wiped."

"And I'm supposed to what? Buy you a friggin' bank? Print the damn money?"

"I don't have a clue...just somethin'. Tell me how to make it go away."

"Is your bill collector a bad guy, a really bad guy?"

"He wants his money, but he's no gangster about to shoot me in the knee cap, if that's what you mean. He knows I'm screwed, just like he is on other properties. Both of us are assholes caught in the run up that's turned into an even faster Space Mountain dive. And his fuckin' weeping is a drag on my sleep...and Nan's."

"How many times did I tell you that accounting was the way to go – not law school, moron. Unless you become a big time corporate lawyer, all you get to see is what the losers do. Being a smart guy, I do the taxes for a couple of dozen or so of my dad's buddies and that's where I see what the smart boys are doing with their money. Some of those old farts have latched onto some real bread in the course of their careers, and I get to peek.

"You got no choice; stop paying on the second and third."

"Thank you, Father Phelan, but you seem to have a bad case of wax buildup. Didn't you hear me say I couldn't pay? They're both months past due, and both of the holders are screaming bloody murder – for me."

"Do they realize that if they foreclose they're going to get zip?"

"They must. They're not moving on me, but the sound effects are driving me nuts. Nan won't even pick up the phone anymore."

"But they're not going to shoot you if you don't pay?"

"No, I don't think so. They're normal stupid shits like me caught in things lots bigger than they understood."

"Go down and get us a couple of brews, I need a minute to run some numbers in my head."

He came back with the beers and sat again. "Well, what do you think?" he asked.

"How about you tell them you can raise ten cents on the dollar and that they have to take it or leave it in full satisfaction of their notes?"

"I like that a lot, but where's the top hat that I'm supposed to pull the rabbit from? Thirty five grand? See; even a lawyer can do ten percent of anything."

"Just do it. If they agree, I'll think of something.

"Oh, if I come up with the dough, the finder's fee is a full partnership in the project. Right?"

"That's easy enough. The project is so far under water that you can have the whole friggin' thing solo. Just make room for the bill collectors in your life…and for their howling at the freakin' moon."

"I'm pretty sure I can come up with the dough. Now get your butt in gear and write up one of those real estate investment trusts with you and Jen as the principals. I've been reading that rental properties are beginning to stabilize ahead of the rest of the housing market and that rents are ripe to be raised.

"If we can get rid of the second and third guys, we can talk the first into reducing and lowering the interest and extending the term to where we could actually make enough to pay the note and our own rent.

"All of them have to know that you've got all the leverage. If you fail, two and three get squat and the bank that holds the first will take a shellacking."

"That sounds great, but what the hell do I really do?"

"Tell that guy in your driveway that, if he shuts up, you'll raise twenty thousand in cash in full satisfaction of his lousy paper...

"Wait! I'm all wrong," I said, "Start with the bank or the guy who holds the first and work your way through the line."

"It's a bank. You think it'll work?"

"How would I know, asshole? You're the guy with the problem. If none of them shoot you, you're home free, and if they do, I'll be a pall bearer. Just don't give them my name; I'm not into pain."

"It has a ring to it; it just might work. Where could you get dough like that?"

"Just do your job and get back to me. I'll deal with the money."

Two days later, I was watching the Nats on the tube when the phone rang; it was Jimmy. "You ain't as dumb as you look, Phelan. All three of them rose up like dolphins in the Baltimore aquarium. I can't believe it; before I could pull my hands back, they snatched the deals. It was like they were waiting for me."

"They were, Jimmy, they were. Tell them you've got the dough lined up and the paperwork will be ready to sign within a week – and they better damn well sign or the deal's off. Tell 'em it'll be all cash and that you'll do the closing in your office."

"You're not shittin' me? You've got it lined up? How'd you do that?"

"Yes! And don't look a friggin' gift horse in the mouth. But not a word to your folks or Nan or your friggin' confessor or anybody else, not even that mongrel cur you call a dog. The guy coughing it up is so quiet you'd think he was dead. Truth of the matter is that I made a good contact at Wells Fargo when I used them to finance this place, so I phoned him about your predicament and my proposed solution. He thought about it and liked it; thought it had some potential.

"He called me back and said he could offer me a small line of credit. So it's done. But the price – besides the dough- is total silence. This isn't the kind of publicity that Wells Fargo would ever need. They're hoping this could be a model, but they'll cut it off at the first sign of trouble – or a leak. You got that?"

"Way to go, Tommy. Hey, they're saving my ass and I'm going on CNN with it? Not likely."

"I'll drop by your office after work next Tuesday with the goods. Set up the transactions any time after that. But like I said, they have to go in order: the first has to agree to his haircut on the debt, the extension and the reduced interest first – without telling two and three; then it's three with two bringing up the rear.

"Remember; if they don't sign the modifications, they are really screwed. Right?"

"Right you are, Tommy. You're the man!"

"Jim, the paper work on the REIT has…"

"The what?"

"The real estate investment trust, the friggin' company that you and Jen will be running. You better start doing your homework on it or we won't get this up and running on time."

"I'm sorry, Tom, I already started researching it. This is all pretty complex stuff. Are there any special things you want covered?"

"Nothing much; we'll be into buying and managing rental properties. I don't know how detailed it has to be, but if you have to, put yourself down as president or managing partner and Jen as chief operating officer. She's been hankering to get a job, and I'm sure she'll like this. If you have to put in numbers – which I doubt - put her down for whatever it takes to use up the thirty thousand we're delivering over the first year. It'll only be part time till we get some projects under management."

"How come Jen and not you?"

"I can't do this and stick with the government. I'd have to quit, and with needy bastards like you hanging around, somebody has to have a job, a real one with actual income."

"You haven't talked with Jen about any of this?"

"It wasn't a go till we locked up the money and you talked those guys out of your wallet. It'll be a surprise but one she'll buy into.

"Hey, date that incorporation ninety days down the road. You can get started without papers. I have to go. Bye, be gone." I said, clearly shutting the door on more questions but quickly added, "By the way, starting right now you've got a new job, too. You have to start lining up management gigs for us. It shouldn't be too hard with all the distressed projects out there and all the jackals from all over the Washington area that'll be hanging around since you announced to your boys that you're dog food."

"Tommy, what's the name of the company?"

"Got a coin?"

"I'll flip it; you call it," Jimmy said as he sent his quarter sailing.

"Tails!"

"You got it."

"`Phelan and Frawley, LLC.' No, `FAF Management '; all Washington companies are three letter jobs."

"What the hell does `FAF Management' stand for?"

"Like I said, `Phelan and Frawley."

"Huh?"

"If `E' can be for Europe and `P' for pneumonia, the `F' can be for Phelan; right?"

"Still an asshole, eh? Some things never change."

As I thought, Jen jumped at the prospect of part time professional employment and a few hours a week away from conjunctivitis central. The idea of working at a banged up spare desk in Jimmy's law office suited her perfectly, and she became the manager of our first property. Even more exciting was the fact that Mom Phelan was thrilled – at least for a time - to be taking care of baby Sean while the older pair was learning to socialize at Happy Acres preschool.

After only three days on the job, Jen announced, "This morning, I went over to the project and introduced myself to all the tenants who were home. Three young housewives and an old retired guy; they were all nice. I told them we were going to get the grounds spruced up and make sure that there was no more trash strewn around. God, they were happy as clams."

"I'm happy for you, Hon; I am. I think we can really do something with this project. We can turn this into a real business with big-time potential."

"Jimmy says that he's getting calls from all over the county from people wanting to talk to him about trying to work out deals."

"I'll just bet they are," I said with a laugh.

On Saturday morning Jimmy dropped by, and I was just starting to talk at the kitchen table with a remarkably recovered and seemingly confident new person who announced, "Tommy, I'm going to have to hire security guards to keep the bastards from breaking down the freakin' door. Everybody's got a project they want FAF to take over."

"You've built a better mousetrap, Frawley, and the whole world is beating a path to your door. Of course it helps a little that the vultures think you've got free cash that they can gobble up, but what the hell, it must be nice to be loved just because you're a sweet person."

"Tommy, you're right; the market may actually be right for projects like ours. And you figured out how to get rid of the excess leverage. This is no bull there are three or four projects that look just like ours did when you rode to the rescue. If you can tap your guy again, we could be in a great situation over the next few years. I mean your formula works like a clock and we could gobble up half a dozen buildings that are ripe for the picking – after we scrape off the slime."

"They'd have to be real clean before my boy would go for it; the bank's already in deep and, according to him, his handlers ain't keeping their nerves secret.

"What's the best you've seen?" I asked.

"There's a project in Springfield on Keene Mill Road not far from Rolling, a garden type group of six buildings pretty much like the one we own – eleven units each, with a full time live in manager who is supposed to be pretty good."

"Yeah, yeah, there's a million of them. Just give me the numbers. What's the real deal?"

"The owner gave a second for half a million. The first is for three point eight mil. The rents are close to covering the first, but the guy's sinking fast. He's got to know if we want it within a couple of weeks."

"What's he want?"

"He says the holder of the second needs a hundred and twenty-five thousand, but I'm sure he'll take less."

"If he wants our dough, he damn well better. What about number one?"

"I'm guessing they'll modify down, give us twenty years and lower the interest to four."

"You've talked with them?"

"No, I'm guessing."

"There'll be no guessing in FAF. My guy won't go for that. I want to take a look at it. If it's half way clean and doesn't look like we'll have to put too much into it, I'll want to see the numbers – really see them. If they check out, then we'll talk, OK?"

"Shit, Tommy, anything you say. You're the man!"

"No, Jimmy, we're the men – FAF, IIM, Ignorant Irish Managers."

By Thursday evening, I was revved up. "OK this looks pretty good; the numbers are pretty much what you said. Your man says he needs a hundred and a quarter, right?"

"Right."

"I've already checked, and if he'll take seventy-five, my guy will bite and take it to his loan committee. But only after the bank – it is a bank, right? - sucks up a half a mil, gives on an extension and lowers the rate – right?"

"Yeah, it's a bank."

"Good. Contact them and then your guy. Give them forty-eight hours each to decide. By the way, that's why Wells Fargo doesn't want any publicity on these deals; they don't want to be seen by other banks as vultures.

"There are plenty of deals, so don't beg; if they don't cave, just walk – no negotiations; it's our way or the highway.

"Call me and I'll get the dough or we'll start all over with other people."

The next day at the office, my phone rang and I saw that it was Frawley. "Jimmy."

"Just like you said."

"OK, bud, write everything up and set up the closings for a week from Monday – separate, of course.

"Meet me at the McDonald's at Kings Park at five o'clock on Friday."

"Order me a Happy Meal," Jimmy said.

Jim was seated at an east side window of the fast food emporium when I spotted him. "No wills or trusts, counselor? You order yet?"

"I just sat down before you got here. And, no, no wills."

I was feeling like a winner and said, "This is a huge day, bud, let's celebrate. I'll have a Big Mac, large fries and the biggest caffeine driven Coke they've got."

"Tommy, it's on me, baby. You're the smartest ignoramus in Virginia. I owe you my friggin' life, man."

"Think nothin' of it, Jimbo. Your day to save mine may well be right around the corner."

Tuesday it was Frawley again, "Right again, Tommy. How did you figure this all out?" he was ecstatic.

"You calling from the office?" I asked.

"No, my car."

"Great, only the whole world can listen in. It's the friggin' money, moron. Nobody but FAF is dumb enough to bring cash to the table. It ain't our brains, it's our Benjamins."

"Yeah, yeah. I got another one, a guy holding a first – alone – called. He's getting a project back for non-payment and wants to give it to us, no money, nothin'; just take it on for the debt. He says he'll even lend us dough at four percent to cover any repairs for the first three years."

"Interesting, but we have to have the numbers. My people are tapped out, except for a small reserve for emergencies. We can't take on much more. We're betting everything on being among the first to spot the turn around, if there really is one coming. If we're off by even six months, we're screwed."

"Whatever you say, Tommy, you've been right every time so far."

"Just fuckin' luck; we're just the only morons doing anything right now. If we're wrong, it'll all be over in a year, and we'll be doing the crying.

"I'll give this one a look, but no matter what, we have to digest what we've got before we take on more. No more deals of any kind, but we'll take on management jobs where everything looks half clean. But no more buys of any kind, even gifts like this one, not even if they pay us to take 'em off their hands."

"Tommy, that's what this last guy is doing."

"Big deal; no friggin' more. If you can get management jobs we can turn this into a perfect circle of tax write downs."

"What's that supposed to mean?"

"We'll write 'em down – accelerated depreciation - and sell 'em to our partners. They'll sell them to our third team, and we'll buy them back at the end of the cycles. It borders on perfect; trust me, Jimmy, perfect."

"I believe, Phelan. Hey, there ain't nobody weeping and wailing in my driveway anymore."

I tried to buck him up with, "It's in your hands, Jimmy. You and Jen have to make this work, but you just can't sit on your asses and watch us grow our way to prosperity. Obviously, everybody in Fairfax County with troubled garden apartments knows you're the go to guy, so just bait and switch 'em into thinking you and Jen can manage their dogs back to health. Just make sure that the projects are fairly clean and that the rents pretty much cover everything – or will once they get the loans modified the way we did ours – with your help, of course – and at a nice fat fee.

"You can do it. Make FAF the hottest idea in Virginia. If I'm right, Jimmy, this window won't be open for more than a few months, so you have to really bust butt to get projects under management. That's as important to this venture as getting our own dogs – which was the easy part."

TWENTY FOUR

B arrow shuffled into my office and closed the door. I rose and watched the ancient skeleton struggle across the floor to the chair fronting my desk and slowly let himself down, virtually falling the last several inches.

"I spoke with HR yesterday. I'm retiring effective at close of business today. I can't do it anymore, Tom, not another minute. I'm fifty seven, and I'd have gone on for a few more years, but I just don't have any strength at all; I'm worn out. I'm sorry."

I couldn't help it as my eyes welled up with tears and I haltingly responded, "No, John, I'm the one who's sorry. You don't owe me a thing. Since this whole thing went down, you've been nothing but kind to me."

Surprisingly, his voice got stronger, "I wish it hadn't begun like it did. I still have all kinds of guilt about dragging you in, but it wasn't me, I swear it. Still, you've supported me in everything around here.

"Would you like me to recommend that you be made acting director? That might give you a leg up when it comes to filling the job permanently."

"That's very kind, but I don't have any interest in the job. Harold's a lot better qualified and I don't want him to think that he has a disgruntled jackass looking over his shoulder. He deserves it, and I don't want it. So just relax. It's you we're worrying about, not me."

"I knew that's how you'd react. You're a good guy. I just hope that everything works as planned."

I tried to reassure him, "Like you said, it borders on perfect, so stop worrying about what's done and can't be changed and concentrate on what's best for Evelyn and you. Call Harold up to your office and tell him that he's your man and that I'll be his humble assistant starting Monday."

On Monday morning, Harold Mortenson came into my office. "Good morning, Tom. Ain't that a god damned shame about John having to retire? That damn smoking, I tried to tell him but it was no use.

"We didn't even have time to take him out for a retirement lunch. I was wondering if you'd mind seeing if we could work something out in a couple of weeks after the dust settles."

"That's a great idea. I'll be glad to check with him and even deliver him to the restaurant.

"So you were nagging him about the weeds, too. It looks like all of us wasted a lot breath on that," I said with disgust.

Just as we turned to the day's business, Pearl knocked and walked in, appearing highly agitated. "Fred Barrow just called. His father died yesterday morning."

I blurted out, "God, not even one workday of retirement. How damn sad is that?"

"He hung in till he was all but dead," Mortenson added.

"Harold, let me know if you ever see that happening to me."

Pearl began to weep, and we both rushed to embrace her. Harold said, "I'm sorry, Pearl; I know how long you worked together and how close you were to him."

She couldn't speak and we half carried her to her chair.

"I'm so sorry, Pearl. He was a great boss," I added.

That Thursday evening when I walked in the door of the funeral home, I could tell almost immediately that John Barrow's wake was a far different affair than Fred Callahan's. I'd seen middle aged cohorts absorb the violent deaths of their friends without flinching. Whether run down, drowned or shot made little difference, it was merely terribly sad and they wept for the widows and half orphans and then returned to their homes and slept soundly. But a premature natural death of a peer frightens them to their cores.

Shifting my glances from face to face, I read the fear in the eyes of the branch chiefs and other fiftyish employees; the corpse in the box could as easily be theirs, and it was clear that they were aware of their mortality. 'Man, they can't react at all; they're scared to death.'

I was in the middle of the division pack as we neared the front of the receiving line, and it appeared that Evelyn and young Fred were quite composed. Unlike most of John's friends, they had had time during the false convalescence to steel themselves for the event.

As I reached her at the head of the line, Evelyn welcomed me, "Thank you for everything, Tom. John said so many times how supportive you were during these last difficult months."

"He changed my life," I said to her, internalizing the multiple meanings of that reply.

The Barrow family gauntlet was far less painful for me than the evening I'd spent in mourning Fred Callahan, and when I gazed at the body, it was amazing to me how much John had shrunk in death. The anxiety that was written on the faces of his older colleagues was now eating at me, and I was beginning to be angry with him for probably leaving me alone to face the shame of being exposed. 'Well, partner, you made it as planned, and on schedule. I may have to do the perp walk out of Belvoir all by myself,' I thought as I counted the seconds for an appropriate contemplation period.

After the respectful moment, I sat down next to Harold. He had tears in his eyes, "He was my first branch chief, Tom, and he gave me every break I ever got in the service. Just before he died, he recommended me for his job to the Chief of Engineers. He was one great guy."

There was no date reserved for the internment of Barrow's soon to be cremated remains in the columbarium at Arlington National Cemetery, so it would be business as usual at the office. The days soon stretched into weeks and months, and the new normalcy of the Mortenson division was at least as quiet and relaxed as that of the previous regime. The division was a well oiled machine that practically ran itself.

My paranoia receded, and I began to think like John that we might all be dead before the FBI started mining the salt dome in Ohio for frauds.

TWENTY FIVE

Jen was stirring the spaghetti sauce and shouting for Ashley to stop teasing Jackie as I tried to watch the evening local news on Channel 4. Jim Vance, the long-time Washington anchor, was describing an undercover sting at the Navy Department that had resulted in the arrest of two Northern Virginia men. I was suddenly focused on the story with laser like precision as Vance described how Mathew Roby, a prominent McLean socialite and philanthropist, and Joseph Johnston, an executive of a successful military contracting company, were arrested as they allegedly entered into a conspiracy to defraud the Navy Department in connection with contracts with Alaskan native corporations.

With the obvious humorous intent of his light sardonic style, Vance noted, "Unfortunately for the hapless pair, the person with whom they were conspiring was in fact an undercover FBI agent.

"Both men are being held in the jail in the Alexandria Federal Courthouse. Prosecutors will ask that both men be held without bail as both are deemed to be flight risks."

"What's the matter, Tommy? You look sick," Jen said as she raced to my side.

I turned to her and mouthed, "I'm fine; just give me a minute. I had a little queasy spell, it's past, everything's fine."

Pulling myself together, I fought for self control and normalcy through dinner and soon found myself bizarrely – hysterically - laughing with the children. "Dinner is the best time of day. Right, Jackie? We eat our din-din together every night, and we have fun and we laugh. Is that what we do while we eat, Ashley?"

Both kids laughed their affirmations, but with a worried look, Jen said, "Are you sure that you're OK, Tommy?"

"Never better, it's just that once in a while, we have to stop to count our blessings. There are no guarantees in life. Right, Love?"

I made a conscious effort to savor the evening activities with the children. "How about Daddy reads you the Big Book of Berenstain Bears before bed tonight?"

Ashley and Jackie yelled and applauded their approval and Sean grinned widely at the animated responses of those who knew what was coming. Ashley added, "Please, Daddy, read the one about the bears go to the doctor."

"You called it; that'll be number one, Honey."

I turned and saw a terribly concerned look on Jen's face, "Why the doom and gloom, Mom? We're having fun; right kids?"

The screams of, "Yes!" guaranteed that it was true.

When I returned to the kitchen after reading about the bears in the rec room and putting the children to bed, Jen turned to me, "What happened?"

"What do you mean? I...don't..."

"You know damn well what I mean. What happened before dinner that made you look like you'd been hit by a truck?"

'It's time,' I thought but just couldn't spill it. "Nothing really, Babe, a passing moment of queasiness and... a little vertigo – it must have been the mystery meat I had for lunch in the cafeteria. It was a wakeup call for me with you and...ah... the kids.

"We all…ah… do things we regret, and that instant was…a… ah… reminder that I wouldn't want to do anything to hurt you or the kids.

"I'd hate to have a heart attack and die without you knowing that despite being a very ordinary man – with all the flaws that go with that…"

"God, Tommy, are you sick, really sick? Are you having chest pains or something?"

"I'm fine…ah…it's just that…I don't take the time…sometimes…to let you know how much I love you. I had that start, and I just wanted to tell you how much you and the kids mean to me."

"Damn it, you're stammering. You only do that when something's totally out of whack. Nothing's so bad that it can't be fixed. Now what the hell's wrong?"

"Just let it go, Jen. It's nothing, but I need you to stop badgering me."

Shaking her head, she turned to do the dinner dishes.

As I dug out the dish towel to do the drying, I felt for a moment that I was going to collapse but fought it off and smiled my way through the chore.

We were all undone by Roby's inability to stop while we had the chance. Without Barrow and me, our scheme at Corps headquarters was no longer viable. The Ft. Belvoir conspiracy had been shut down and I alone remained in the office.

As Barrow predicted and I agreed, Roby could never quit, so the Navy was his next port of call. 'Anchors aweigh and hello Bubba,' was my depressing thought, 'Obviously, my perp walk was in the process of being scheduled for Monday.'

TWENTY SIX

After all of my years at Belvoir, all that I had to pack up were two family photos: one of Jen and the kids, and the other a portrait of my mother and father taken at about the time of their twenty-fifth wedding anniversary. My first task that Monday morning was to save them, the representational them. After sliding the portraits into my brief case, I had to sit for a moment to regain my composure.

Gathering myself, I walked out into the outer office and said, "Pearl, I have to go out to my car for a minute. If anyone calls, I'll be right back."

As I placed the brief case in the trunk carefully and softly, I whispered, "You could all be lost when this goes down. I didn't want that to happen."

Walking slowly back into the office, I sat and pretended to read a memo that I'd drafted on Friday, but in reality my focus was on the door to the corridor just beyond Pearl's desk.

My assessment of what would transpire was on the money. I happened to check my watch at nine-twelve and on looking up saw three uniformed security guards and two men in civilian clothes – dark pinstripe suits - march into the office and approach Pearl. I couldn't hear what they said but had no doubt about what was happening as she turned and pointed at me. The two civilians led the entourage into my office.

The bullet headed, bull necked older member of the pair was clearly in charge, "Thomas Phelan?"

"Yes, sir."

Flashing his identification, the man recited, "I'm Farley Cooper, Special Agent of the Federal Bureau of Investigation. I have here a warrant for your arrest for committing fraud against the government of the United States and for conspiracy to commit fraud against the government of the United States," and he held out the paper for examination.

I gently accepted the paper and began to read it.

He continued, "Mr. Phelan, You are under arrest. You have the right to remain silent. Anything you say or do can and will be held against you in a court of law. You have the right to speak to an attorney. If you cannot afford an attorney, one will be appointed for you.

"Do you understand these rights as they have been read to you?"

Amazingly, for a split second my mind was focused better than I ever remember, and the magnitude of what was happening was clear. At almost the same time, two streams of consciousness were racing through my mind: in one my role in the conspiracy was instantly minimized and blame for what was happening was being spread generously over Matt and Amanda and John Barrow; in the other I was naked in my guilt before Jen and my folks.

But I had to react to the warrant and did, "Yes, sir, I do, and I wish to invoke my right to remain silent – at this time. So before answering any questions or making any further comments, I wish to speak to my attorney. His name is James Frawley of Fairfax, Virginia."

I felt my face flush when I saw the look of horror on the faces of Pearl and Harold in the background, but I had rehearsed this scene so many times in my head that as Cooper placed the cuffs on my wrists, I was as prepared as possible for my walk of shame. As we filed out of the office with Cooper and me leading the way, and at the sight of my two long time co-workers and – former – friends covering their mouths in horror, my shame was overwhelming. 'Fucking John knew enough to start smoking early into this shit. He should have been the grand marshal of this friggin' parade,' I thought as I worked to shift my guilt into outrage for the dead man.

My new life was underway and by two o'clock that afternoon my shocked attorney was in the midst of his first interview with me.

The monologue that I'd rehearsed so many times in my head was in great form and almost completed, "So that's it, Jimmy. I was entrapped, blackmailed and felt physically threatened. I knew it was wrong, criminal, so after a couple of fits and starts in trying to launder the money, my conscience was killing me, but I didn't know what to do or where to turn. At the time, I was afraid for my life and of being exposed for what I'd done in Mexico, and the only thing I could think of was to never again touch the money for my own use and when the conspiracy was undone – which I fully expected - to give it all back and to cooperate fully with the prosecutors and police."

My role fully played, I changed the subject, "Remember when I told you that you'd have your chance to save my life, well here it is. What do I do now?"

Jimmy appeared stunned, "Good Jesus, Tommy, you're in shit up to your fuckin' eyeballs. Man, you need a friggin' lawyer - bad."

In spite of the predicament, I burst out laughing, "But that's why you're here, Jimbo."

Still obviously reeling at the magnitude of what I'd just confessed, he said, "You don't get it, Tommy; I appeal breathalyzer results and challenge radar gun calibrations. I write wills and trusts. You're in here for felonies that could land you in a federal pen for half your friggin' life. You need a lawyer, a real freakin' lawyer - right freakin' now!"

Knowing this was coming for months, without panic, I asked, "You know the right one?"

"I know a couple of really good ones, if they're available."

"Well get one of them down here right away. And you're still with me - co-counsel. I won't hire one of them, if they won't let you stick with me. That's a must. Got it?"

"That's the best example of misplaced trust I've ever come across, moron. And it drives up your costs."

"Not as much as you think. I'm going to sing like a horny bird in springtime and deal like a table man in Vegas. I was entrapped, blackmailed and my life was under threat. How bad can it really be?"

"Are you shittin' me? You're looking at gray hair in the can," Frawley was clearly agitated to the point of hysteria. "Ah, what the fuck, you want me in, I'm in."

"Good man! OK, Jimmy that was the easy part. Now you really have to save my life. You have to go out there and face Jen and buffer me. This is going to be the worst meeting of my life, and you have to soften her up so I don't die of a heart attack in this hole."

"I'll try," he said looking like I'd broken his heart.

"No; you'll pull it off. By now, you've got it – entrapped, blackmailed and in fear for my life, a beautiful triplet. You have to make her see how bad my situation was. I couldn't see any other way; I may have been blind and wrong, but I honestly saw no other way.

"I can't be the one who explains it from the start, Jim. It will kill me if Jen hasn't been made to see that I was entrapped into what happened in Cancun. You have to hint at what happened without really saying it. It would kill her – and me.

"The same goes for my folks. You know that their lives have always been based on honesty and integrity – and the Golden Rule. You have to get to them before they see me in here.

"I can't face them unless you do this for me, Jim. I've never needed you to come through for me like I need you now. You'll save me; right?"

"Damn, Tom, I'm a loser, but I really will try to come through for you on this one."

"Loser, my ass. When I met you in first grade, I knew you'd have my back for life.

"For years – since Barrow told me how it was going to be - I knew I'd have to face Jen and the folks in the worst moments of my life. But deep down, I fantasized that you'd make it possible for my life – all of our lives - to go on after it happened. Win this one for me and I'll never forget it, Jim, never, ever."

"Tommy, what about the business, our business? What do…"

"That's all irrelevant; it has nothing to do with what I'm in here for. You got that? Nothing. Forget about it."

"Whatever you say; you're the one in the slammer."

"You got it. Now go face my music… and get that damn real lawyer of yours down here yesterday."

Half an hour later, I sat alone in the bare room waiting for Jen and became conscious that a metal table and three metal chairs were the only items in the locked space. Like the furniture, the walls, ceiling and concrete floor were all painted battleship gray. There was a window about one foot square in the top half of the metal door that was clearly reinforced with some sort of cross wiring designed to prevent fragmentation in case someone struck it with a chair or a shoulder. 'Cowardly Tommy Phelan has no intention of hurting his shoulder on that baby,' was the thought that crossed my mind when I spotted Jen at the door in the company of a uniformed bailiff.

'Give me strength!' I prayed.

I heard the click and the door opened. It closed and clicked again behind her as she started toward me. Already weeping when she reached to embrace me, she said softly, "I would have understood; I would have. You should have trusted me… had faith in me. God, you're locked up in this damned dungeon. What are we going to do, Tommy?"

Embracing her, I said, "It will all work out. I'm so sorry, Jen. You were right from the beginning. Roby was only out to use me, and I was blinded by discontent with my job."

"I love you, Tommy. I need…we all need you. You're innocent! You are, aren't you?"

"I am! And I love you, too. I was blackmailed into cooperating with Roby. Every rotten penny is going to be returned, and I'm finally free to tell the truth, my side of the whole mess. Everything is going to be fine, just like before, Jen."

"Jimmy says he has a terrific lawyer to defend you and to get you out of here."

"That's great. Are the kids alright?"

"Of course; they're too young to be aware of anything. Your Mom and Dad are at the house with them. They're putting up a brave front, but they're hurting bad, Tommy, real bad.

"Jimmy said he'd go by on his way home and tell them the straight story. He told me that you had no choice, they would have killed you."

"Sit down, Hon," I said as we slowly released each other. "I should have listened to you. You saw from the start that there was something rotten about them and that I should have walked away. But I was so unhappy with my future with the government that I was blind to what I was up against until it was too late.

"But Jimmy says I'm OK; that I'll be out of here in nothing flat.

"So tell Mom and Dad that it'll all work out. Try not to let them come down here. I don't want them seeing me in here. Tell them I really am a good man, a good son, that I was entrapped and threatened, that I had no choice. Tell them I love 'em and that I'll be free very soon. Tell them."

We rose and embraced desperately.

"I'll tell them; I will."

That night shortly after nine, I was finishing up with my new counsel. "That's it, Mr. Stetson: entrapped, blackmailed and physically threatened. I was never so scared in my life. I…"

"Call me Charles, Tom. We're going to be working together for a long time. The facts are clear. Obviously you're not going to run and you pose no threat to yourself or the community. I'm certain that the prosecutors will see a significant difference in your situation from those of Roby and Johnston, so I'm sure that we'll be able to get you out of here in nothing flat, probably before noon tomorrow.

"Beyond that, your story is compelling: all the money returned; total cooperation with the investigation; absolute innocence on the conspiracy charges…with unassailable evidence; and fear for your life and the lives of your loved ones. You have a lot going for you, Tom.

"We'll be attending a bail hearing later, and I'm sure that the amount of the bond will not be excessive or beyond your ability to raise it.

"Questions?"

"Do you think that I'll have to go to prison?"

"I wouldn't want to be the prosecutor watching you tell your story to a jury, so there's no doubt in my mind that your bargaining position is as strong as any case of this type that I've ever handled.

"In promising full restitution of such a huge sum, your credibility is very high. That's a token of your basic honesty and full cooperation. But you're not to answer any questions until I give you the go ahead. Clear?"

"Crystal."

"Wonderful; now rest easy; you're innocent and I'm on your case."

Waiting for my father – naturally it would take more than wishful thinking and a personal request that he not come to see me in jail, I felt that I could begin to breathe normally, seemingly for the first time since seeing the TV clip about Matt Roby's arrest. 'I lived through the meeting with Jen, and I'm beginning to believe that I can survive the one with Pat.' "But maybe not; oh, man," I whispered.

Seated on a bench, my father waited for me as I walked down the corridor in the jail. He rose and tears filled his eyes as we came together in a powerful embrace. "I'm so sorry, Tom. Why didn't you confide in me? I'd have moved heaven and earth to help you out of the mess."

"I know, but I got caught up in some pretty rough stuff in Mexico, and I was ashamed, and then I was trapped and thought that Jen and the kids might be in danger. It was all a blur and I just didn't know what to do.

"Thanks for posting my bond. I'll pay you back. Thank God the judge believed me; the damn prosecutor wanted half a million."

"Oh, I know you'll take care of it, but we'd have made it somehow or other. As it is, the cost of the bond's hardly anything on fifty thousand. But that's the least of our troubles, so stop worrying about the small stuff," he said and then tried to lighten the situation with, "But, if you don't mind, please don't think of running; Mom and I like the house, and we had to post it as collateral," and finished with a forced laugh.

Serious again, he said, "Your lawyer – Stetson, right? – he seems sharp?"

"As a tack."

"Mom's still at your place. She's all clued in, so don't go getting her too upset. You're home; you're innocent; and you're going to beat this.

TWENTY SEVEN

Several weeks after my arrest, a meeting at Stetson's office brought the status of my plea bargain up to date. "The prosecutors are sticking with their demand for a felony conviction on one count of fraud. They say that their bottom line is six months in jail and two and a half years of supervised probation. Naturally – and as we've already agreed – you have to continue to cooperate fully and testify against Roby and Johnston. I think we should buy the conviction and just stick with the present thinking on no jail time. "

"I'm with you all the way on the no jail time, Charles, but I had no choice on the whole operation, and I really don't want to agree to plead guilty to a felony. I'll lose my civil rights, and carrying the title of `convicted felon' for the rest of my life doesn't sound real good to me. I'm innocent and willing to go to trial. After all, I'm paying another mighty high price in that I'll never be able to hold another government job – or any job that pays anywhere near what I was making."

"I don't think that's the way to approach this, Tom. I think we can get them down to a few months of house arrest that will let you work at your wife's company. It sounds like she and Jim Frawley have something pretty good going with those apartment complexes and that you'd be a welcome employee. You said that you're already rather heavily involved."

I felt that I couldn't let Stetson carry the day, and I sure didn't want him to think that I'd bought into his logic. "I can't believe that they're demanding a felony conviction."

"Tom, let me be very candid; your position that your life and the lives of your wife and children were threatened, while rightly powerful to you, isn't swaying the prosecutors at all. They're confident that they will be able to tear it apart for a jury. They flat out told me that they'll attack that point without mercy."

"Let them try walking in my shoes. Let me tell you the threat was very real when I thought of my kids. I…"

Stetson soothed me, "I know, but it's not me that you have to convince. If you take the stand, they'll tear you apart. If you don't, they'll mock you.

"From their perspective, you could've come forward at any point and closed the case in one day. The FBI would have had Roby off the street and in a jail before any threats could've been carried out, and he's going to prison for so long that anything he had in mind for you would have to be carried out from a wheelchair or a walker.

"While the mitigating circumstances are clear to you – and me – and would no doubt be taken into account in sentencing, you could very well be facing serious time behind bars. If you wound up serving time even in a minimum security facility, I'd be failing you by not pointing out the danger."

"I have to sleep on it. I see where you're coming from, Charles, but I really think the system isn't treating me right."

"Of course, but my advice isn't designed to get you justice; it's to get you out of this mess with the least possible damage to you. Frankly, your situation looks very bright. Jenifer has an up and coming business and is already using your expertise to great advantage. If you were to get house arrest with the right to go to work, it would be nothing more than a slap on the wrist.

"If we go to trial and – heaven forbid – you wind up with time in prison, plus long term probation, that would be a terrible blow to both of us. I hate to implore you on personal grounds, but I have a lot more experience in plea bargaining than you. I think that a betting man would like the odds on house arrest against possibly real time in a penitentiary and only an outside chance of being found innocent and walking out of court a free man."

To say that I was depressed while driving home from Stetson's office would be a gross understatement.

The next morning I found myself in one of the examining rooms in the Federal Courthouse with Farley Cooper, now representing the U.S. Attorney's office for my case, and he was as every bit as charming as he'd been at the arrest, "Let me get this straight, Sunshine, you and Barrow disliked each other, right?" he snarled at me with what I interpreted to be complete contempt.

"That's right. He helped drag me into the ring and at first I hated him for it. He sensed it and returned the favor, over time we came to develop a working relationship – had to or the whole thing would have collapsed."

"Now wouldn't that have been too bad for an innocent like you intent on doing the right thing?

"How do you account for the fact that everybody who knew both of you at Fort Belvoir, and even Barrow's widow, thought that you and Barrow had practically a father and son relationship?"

"We had jobs to do if the enterprise wasn't going to come undone, so we sucked up our personal animosity to the degree needed to survive."

"You don't really expect me to believe the bull crap that you were afraid for your life?"

"It's true; Barrow was frightened to death of Roby. John was convinced that Roby had contracted to have Callahan killed and would do the same to him – and me - if we didn't go along."

Instantly Cooper was transformed into Mr. Hyde, eyes bulging, face on fire and his bull neck swollen. "What unadulterated bullshit! Roby had nothing to do with Callahan's death and you both knew it."

"That's not true. And let me tell you, Barrow quaked in his boots whenever we talked about Roby's ruthlessness in running the operation."

"Let me get this straight; you're throwing your boss, your mentor and –really – your friend under the bus to save your useless ass. Years of conspiracy and solidarity be damned; he's dead and being chucked out the window just because it's better for you. My God, you have no character whatsoever, Phelan. I've taken dozens of low lifes with more guts and character than you off the streets, and not one of them ever stooped that low. You're lower than a snake in the grass."

"I'm telling you the truth."

"Well you've got brass balls. So let me get this straight; you had to cooperate with Roby? You had to start laundering money or be killed? You only became a felon because Roby made you one? My God, Phelan you must have been hell on teachers when you told them that your dog ate your homework. Well hear this:

this isn't junior high school and I don't believe a single goddamn word of your cock and bull story."

"It's true; I swear it."

"If you think for one minute that I'm going to tell the prosecutors that you're cooperating and that you should get your plea deal, you're the biggest moron on the planet. You're a lying, swindling sack of shit and you were a crook from the get go.

"Now one more time from the top; where's the goddamn money?"

"You guys have all of the money I ever received from Roby – every dime - and that is the truth."

Cooper was standing menacingly at my shoulder, and the arteries at his temples were popping with every heartbeat. "You're making me sick to my stomach, you lying crook. Between Callahan and Barrow there's still a barrel of dough missing – maybe half a million, maybe even a million or more. And you, you son-of-bitch, I know that you've got it."

"That's crazy! I didn't know anything about the scam until after Callahan was dead. Why would he ever involve me in the thing? And if they had Callahan's cut, why would Roby and Barrow ever let me have a sniff of it? Barrow and I had only a working relationship, and I never knew anything about him or his money.

"Why don't you ask the families," I said in frustration.

"Don't worry; the government is going to get plenty more blood from those turnips than you'll ever believe, but I don't think for a minute that they had anything to do with the fraud – or the missing money. I think that you're a sly little bastard who thinks he can get away with this caper. You fell into a bucket of shit and you're intent on coming out smelling like a rose. The two guys who knew your role in this syndicate were loyal enough to you to croak before I could get my hands on them, and you, lying sack of manure that you are, can slander them with impunity. You are one fortunate bastard, Phelan, but I'm wise to you and haven't even begun to grind you.

"Roby says that it's most likely you who has the missing cash. And I think so, too," the last sentence was said with great malevolence.

I was sweating and finding it more difficult to control my own anger, "Mr. Cooper, I'm really trying to cooperate; you and I both know that my freedom is at stake. That last whopper by Roby makes no sense whatsoever. You've acknowledged that he didn't know anything about what went on in Belvoir. Frankly, he didn't give a crap about any of us. He set the operation up with Callahan and had Barrow – and me - fingered for entrapment and blackmailing. That he wasn't a physical danger to us wasn't ever obvious till late in the game...and really not even then. And let me tell you, Roby wasn't above hinting at threats, not that he ever really said anything specific. As far…"

"As far, my ass; I know you've got the dough, and I'm going to get it from you and make sure you spend a dozen years in prison for lying to a federal officer."

I shook my head, "I don't get it; is this just some crazy interrogation technique? You don't have anything – nothing - to back up this ridiculous theory. I confessed immediately; I gave back every dime that I ever collected. You've seen the video that they used to trap me, and you know damn well I'm telling the truth. I'll bet that Roby has admitted as much, and still you're treating me like it was all my idea."

"I know it wasn't your idea, Phelan, but I'm convinced that you've got the missing dough and that you think you're going to get away with it. Trust me, it ain't gonna happen. I'll haunt you for the rest of your useless life till I get it – and put you away."

"Mr. Cooper, I've done some things in my life that I'm not proud of and getting sucked into this mess is the worst and most obvious, but I'm cooperating with you because I want this to be over in the best way possible for me and my family. I'm telling you the truth."

"Get this straight, Phelan. You can cry and moan till the cows come home, but I'm never going to believe you, never! Never; you got that? There's no damn hurry on this plea. I can haul you down here every week for the rest of my career and will until you cough up that money."

Without a pause, Copper changed the subject, "How come you were brought into Callahan's branch?"

I took a deep breath and readied for a change of direction in his assault, "One of the contracting officers retired, and the contracts I was managing in my old branch were more like those in Callahan's branch than most of the other junior people in the division, and Barrow and Callahan approached me with the idea of the switch. I thought it wasn't a bad move, so I agreed. It's as simple as that. And looking back, I don't have any reason to think otherwise."

"Yeah, right," was Cooper's caustic reaction.

"I'm telling you; that's all there was to it. Unless you have a theory that now goes to Barrow and Roby plotting Callahan's hit and run, nothing else makes any sense. You're being ridiculous on this."

"I'll determine what's ridiculous. Your job is to cooperate; you signed on to do it. And frankly, I don't see any of that."

After well over an hour of this browbeating, I stopped for a couple Samuel Adams Boston Lagers before driving to Stetson's office to vent. "That damn Cooper's killing me, Charles. No matter what I say, he's in my face like a maniac calling me a liar and worse. He says he's going to scuttle the plea agreement and hound me till I confess to knowing where the missing money from Callahan and Barrow is. I didn't have a clue that there was a criminal enterprise until long after Callahan was dead, and Barrow – in our few civil moments - hinted that it was all tied up in art investments. He sure as hell wasn't interested in making me his damn beneficiary."

"I know, I know. I've been involved with Cooper a number of times in the past, and he's a miserable person, a bully who's had success at browbeating the truth out of people. It works, so they use him and he does it.

"The prosecutors like to have him on cases like yours where they have weak positions; he occasionally pulls their rabbits out for them. Just stick to your guns with the truth and it will all work out.

"You'll just have to suffer through it. The prosecutors are closing in on house arrest and probation. I sure hope that you are, too. You are, aren't you, Tom?"

I couldn't answer the question in the state I was in. "Can't you get him off my back? He's got nothing, but he keeps on grinding me."

"I can't do a thing about him. The prosecutors love him and won't interfere.

"You are giving the plea bargain thought aren't you?" he asked again.

After a long pause, I said, "Yes," with obvious reluctance.

"Good man; it won't be long before we put this two bit Javert back in his box…"

"Javert? What's that?"

"You've seen Les Mis. He's the cop who torments Jean Valjean all of his life."

"Oh, yeah; that's the son of a bitch alright," I said and chuckled, "but it's not funny; Cooper is one miserable bastard."

"Don't worry, the prosecution has to fish or cut bait on a speedy trial and Cooper has only a short time to work his magic. Just bear with it; it'll all be over soon."

Stetson returned to his theme, "In short order, you're going to have to face up to a plea or a trial. You know where I stand, very strongly in favor of avoiding a trial. Don't let pride stand in the way of your freedom. You're not like most people accused of crime; you did participate in the enterprise, but your story on being entrapped and blackmailed is really solid, even Roby admits to it. That you were afraid for your life is pretty darn strong too, but you continued in the enterprise when you knew – or should have known - that you could have turned him in and been protected by the feds. You…"

"Charles, you have to see…"

"Tom what I have to see is immaterial. It's what a jury would see. Your story is compelling but don't forget what happened to Patty Hearst. You remember that old Black Panther case; she suffered far more brutal coercion than you can even imagine. And she was convicted and sent to prison. Now don't do anything on principle that will get you in more trouble than you're already in."

Without waiting for an answer, Stetson closed the session. "You know the facts and the odds. You'll be called upon to make up your mind very shortly. Be ready."

"Don't worry, I'll be ready. I've got to go."

That night at the house, they had me surrounded. "Damn it, I'm innocent; why are all of you pushing me to plead guilty? I was frustrated facing Jen and my folks in the living room. "There'll be a stigma that will be with me – with all of us…and the kids – for the rest of our lives."

My Dad was forcing his way into the lead, "Stetson says that the odds of you being found guilty are damn high – almost certain. You know his arguments better than we do, but they sure scare the crap out of me.

"The deal he's got practically sewed up has you home in your bed every night and working with Jen and Jimmy every damn day. You're going to bet that against a conviction and maybe a year – or more - in federal prison because you don't see it that way? Come on, Tommy, you're not thinking straight."

"But I want a chance to clear my…"

"Tommy, that chance could blow up in your face." Jen interjected. "Jimmy completely agrees with Stetson. Be sensible. We've got a good thing going with FAF, and it's all your doing. The way things are going, your income will be made up in just a matter of months – not years. The people in this room think that you're innocent. We're the only ones who really care about you and don't care at all about what other people think."

Mom chimed in, "They're talking sense, baby; listen to Dad and Jen. We're all on your side, and we think you'll be making a big mistake if you fight this for the sake of pride. Remember, Tommy, pride goeth before the fall. Tommy, please listen to them," she said. "Now tell us that you will."

I went into an out and out tirade of minor profanity before saying, "Alright, goddamn it."

"Thanks be to God!" Mom said as she dropped into the nearest easy chair.

TWENTY EIGHT

Stetson and Jimmy were with me in the hallway outside of the courtroom, and Charles was leading the discussion; actually he was beating me up, "The prosecutors won't budge on the six months of house arrest and thirty months of supervised probation, and that's not a big deal. They started with eighteen months in prison, five years of probation and a quarter of a million dollar fine, but when the forensic audit came back and showed that you'd returned two hundred dollars more than was given to you, they began to backtrack. The deal they're offering amounts to a victory for us – virtual vindication.

"Please, Tom, don't say a word that will upset the applecart. They've been getting all kinds of grief from that jackass Cooper. They're really treating us right in saying that you've been open and cooperative, so don't start complaining about the unfairness of life. Just take this gift and walk out of here a free man."

Jimmy chimed in, "God damn it, Tommy; he's right; this is the one minute in your life that you have to keep your smart ass mouth shut. 'Yes, sir; no, sir, three bags full, 'is all that we want to hear from you. Jen is supposed to drive you home in twenty minutes, but I have this friggin' fear that you're going to fuck up the plea, and the judge is going to order you to stand trial. Tell me that I'm crazy, Tommy, tell me."

My head hanging, I replied, "I'm in. You can count on me."

Charles checked his watch and announced, "OK we're up." And we pulled ourselves to full height and marched into the courtroom like three proud horses in a troika.

Man, was I was relieved when I surveyed the scene and saw only three people, Jen and my folks, in the spectators' section. Aside from uniformed bailiffs and obvious support staff, there were several men in business suits at the front whom I didn't recognize but whom I assumed to be the prosecuting team. I thanked God that there was no friggin' sign of Cooper in the courtroom.

One of the bailiffs announced the judge and we all rose to honor him and to begin the proceedings.

The judge announced that the court docket was extremely busy, so he was going to be very direct. "Mr. Phelan, are you aware that the plea submitted in your name will require you to plead guilty to a felony?"

"Yes, Your Honor."

"You know that being a convicted felon will impact your civil rights in some ways for your entire life? Have you been fully briefed on what all of this means by your counsel?"

"I am aware, and I have been fully briefed, Your Honor."

"Are you aware that you will be unable to change your plea if and when this agreement is accepted by the court and affirmed by you?"

"Yes, Your Honor."

"I have studied the briefs and agree with the attorneys for both sides that the plea submitted would result in a reasonable disposition of the case and be in the best interests of both the government and the defendant. You are to be charged with one felony count of fraud against the government of the United States. If you plead guilty, you will be sentenced to six months of house arrest with permission to drive to and from your place of employment and perform the normal work associated with the employment listed in the plea. In addition you will be sentenced to thirty months in a federal prison. That portion of the sentence will be suspended and you will be placed on probation for a period of that same thirty months. Failure to abide by the terms of the probation will result in you being remanded to the custody of the Federal Bureau of Prisons to serve of the remainder of your sentence.

"Do you understand these terms and are you willing to abide by them?"

"Yes, Your Honor."

"Questions or comments from the government?"

"None, Your Honor"

"Mr. Stetson?"

"No, Your Honor."

"Mr. Phelan, do you have any questions?"

"None, Your Honor."

"Thomas Phelan, you are charged with fraud against the government of the United States. How do you plead?"

"Guilty as charged, Your Honor."

"In accordance with the terms and conditions agreed to by the government and the defense, I sentence you to the punishment previously discussed.

"Do wish to address the court, Mr. Phelan?"

I cleared my throat and watched as Charles and Jimmy began to squirm, "Your Honor, I just want to say that I'm sorry for what

I did and for not being bolder in trying to thwart the criminal enterprise. I knew that it was wrong from the beginning, and I'm deeply ashamed of what I did and did not do."

"Your predicament was difficult, Mr. Phelan, but your actions were not without rationality, even some merit. I believe that the resolution is equitable.

"Case closed."

After the judge departed, Jimmy said softly, "I never would have believed that you could do that without going seriously off message, Tommy. Will wonders never cease?"

"I'll see you at work in the morning, and we will discuss that comment, counselor," I said with false malevolence.

As soon as the door to the judge's chamber closed, I and the three spectators made mad dashes into a loving scrum. "Tommy, you're free. We can go home," Jen said in obvious relief.

My dad said nothing but patted my back and Mom openly wept. "I prayed for this, Tommy. All of us will be sleeping in our own beds tonight with no more worries about this terrible experience."

When we arrived at the office, it was all smiles, but on the way home reality set in. I was driving and tried to continue the happy banter that had been the order of the day, but Jen did not pick up on it.

She spoke slowly, somberly and softly, "I'm very disappointed in you, Tommy. You betrayed me; you betrayed all of us – the kids… your folks. Your vows meant nothing to you. You've poisoned the well. Things will never be the same between us again."

My first thought was to blow up in anger and shout her down, but, thank God I was able to hold my tongue and to follow the better path of begging forgiveness and seeking sympathy.

"I swear to God, Jen, it meant nothing. They got me blind drunk and when my defenses were down, I was entrapped into the mess," I said with all the sincerity that I could muster.

I knew that her wounds were real but there was a lot of – well more than a little - truth on my side. I also felt that my response was the best I could have made, as I was sure that she would have blown up with rage had I even hinted at a more aggressive tack.

Her silence was the signal to me that our marriage could be made whole again – maybe even happy, but I knew then that I was on double probation and would be for an indeterminate period. But despite this setback it was one of the great days in the life of Tommy Phelan, I had gone a whole day without being totally stupid and recognized that this was the first day of my new life.

TWENTY NINE

"The furnace in unit one on Route 236 went out last night. We've got to get somebody out there this morning. How're we going to pay for it?" Jimmy asked.

"What are we talking about here – two…five…ten thousand?" I said.

"I'm guessing closer to fifteen," Jen said. She was FAF's Chief Operating Officer and was showing an early talent for management.

"I hate to go into hock for something that small but we can't let it go and ignoring maintenance in general will create even more headaches down the road.

"Tell you what, my Wells Fargo guy will probably buy into this one, but based on strong hints the last time I spoke with him, I'm pretty sure that this will tap them out – at least until they determine that we can really pull this act off. I'll beg, borrow or steal this fifteen from him and check where we stand with them.

"So, Jen, make some calls and find out who's good and reasonable and get them out there – pronto. In the meantime, you guys keep all this under your hat. With no more banking sugar daddy, we're about to be on our own."

"OK, Tommy; makes sense; I'm on it," she said.

I was constantly amazed at how close to insolvency FAF was running, but I could also see that Jimmy, Jen and my dad were growing in confidence that our basic plan was pretty sound. I kept preaching that if we could hang in a year or two we could turn the corner and leverage the whole shebang into a fortune that could actually turn us into the big time capitalists John Barrow had envisioned.

I was also aware that they skirted around all money issues and did exactly as I said and never questioned where it was all coming from; Wells Fargo indeed.

The next week, as I entered the office of my probation officer, Franklin Jackson, for the first time, I was shocked to find Agent Farley Cooper sitting in one of the two chairs in front of Jackson's desk. "Welcome to the world of probation, Sunshine. Sit down and make yourself comfortable; it's great you're aware that your continuing cooperation with the government is essential if your probation is not to be revoked, so I thought I'd come over and initiate you to your new status."

Mr. Jackson said, "Have a seat, Phelan."

Seated in the other chair and mesmerized by the situation, I didn't say a word…but was mighty damned anxious to say the least.

Ignoring Jackson, Cooper continued his monologue, "I'll be with you over the coming years and will report regularly to the court on your cooperation. My reports will go to both the U.S. Attorney's office and directly to the judge, so no matter what the chicken shit prosecutors think, they'll have no impact on what the judge sees. So just because those `Nervous Nellies' were afraid they might lose the case if they didn't cave to you and Stetson, they won't have any role in filtering out the truth in what the judge gets to see about your cooperation from my perspective.

"So instead of getting sanitized reports on your cooperation from the Justice Department lawyer flunkies, the judge will get what he needs to see you for what you are: a damn con man and swindler, trying to get away with a barrel of government dough."

I tried to control my anger but couldn't help contemptuously blurting out, "I'll do my best to answer all of your questions fully and truthfully."

"I'll bet you will, you lying sack of shit. OK, Sunshine; question one: where's the damn money."

"I told you before; every dime I got out of the enterprise was turned over to the government."

"You hear that bullshit, Frank? By the time his probation's up, I'm going to find the other couple of million he's got squirreled away under some rock in Fairfax, and he'll be pulling eight to ten in Leavenworth," Cooper cackled with obvious delight at his performance.

"Well I have to go, but I'll be back…again and again" Copper said with a malevolent grin as he rose to leave.

When the door closed, Jackson turned to me, "I don't know anything other than what's in the case file. Your job is to abide fully and completely with the terms of the probation order. You do that and we'll get along fine. You are going straight to and from work, right? No stops for a beer after work? Nothing?"

"Yes, sir. I just want you to know that I fully cooperated with the gov…"

"Phelan, that's between you, the court and Cooper. I won't put any more weight on what he says about you than I will on what you say about him. Clear?"

"Yes, sir."

"Good. I'll see you here every second and fourth Tuesday at ten sharp. Give me plenty of notice, if you're going to need to make a change. And don't even think about being too sick to make it here; only admission to a hospital or a note from the medical examiner on how you croaked will cut it.

"Phelan, you've got the easiest row to hoe I've come across in a long time. Don't screw it up."

"I won't, sir."

"Very well, you're done; I have a lot of cases to deal with. See you next time."

"Yes, sir," I said while almost levitating from the chair and hustling out of the office.

THIRTY

Six months of house arrest was a pain, as I had no excuses for not being available for duty as a house husband and yard boy. I suspected, however, that it was probably a lot easier than doing Bubba's shirts in the prison laundry. But I made it through with my marriage in better shape than when I started. Halleluiah!

Two weeks after completing my required confinement to quarters, Jen and I found ourselves stuck in heavy traffic on the way to the office. The radio reporter indicated that there were jams all over Northern Virginia, and the problems at the intersection of Braddock Road and Route 123 were apparently typical for the day. While sitting and stewing, I decided that it would be a good day to make a move on the last of Barrow's money in the storage unit.

Turning to her, I said, "I'll drop you off at the office. Our main money man works in the Lorton Branch of Wells Fargo and – given this traffic - it's for sure that he won't be out gallivanting, so I think that I'll run down and update him on what we're doing in buying up rentals.

"Tell Jimmy I won't be in till afternoon. I'll grab a sandwich in the cafeteria of the art center at Lorton, so don't wait for me."

"Do you want me to go with you?"

I knew she had her doubts about the money but I wasn't about to compromise her, "Nah, waste of time; just keep bugging that lawn care guy to get cracking. All the projects are looking ratty, and if he wants to keep the contract, he damn well better start putting some resources into the job."

I pulled up to the office condo on Judicial Drive and, after giving her a kiss, I took off for the stash. Looking at her through the rearview mirror, I said quietly, "She damn well knows…suspects. What the hell; it borders on perfect; how damn true."

Talking my way into the storage facility, I quickly opened my unit and yanked the two aluminum suitcases out and flipped them into the trunk. Looking around carefully, I whispered, "Last roundup, little doggies."

After wasting a half an hour at the old prison turned art center gobbling down a chicken sandwich on hard, dry white bread, I drove toward Fairfax in the right lane of Ox Rd., making sure that the pace was slow enough to cause everyone to pass me, often to the tune of horns that were usually accompanied by finger waves. When I was sure that there was no car in sight maintaining my ridiculous pace, I accelerated to the speed of the traffic and headed for the house where, after checking for walkers, I casually placed the two travel bags in the carport overhead and guessed from the weight and a quick glance that there wasn't much more than fifty thousand dollars.

Quickly changing my mind, I climbed back up in the overhead and hauled the treasure down, and, carried it into the basement to begin the final inventory. "Fifty-eight thousand, two hundred bucks. Shit, I could have passed this for gas and bread."

Loading the money into a small cardboard box, I placed it on the shelf with the leftover cans of paint.

Tossing the emptied travel bags into the back seat, I drove to the Salvation Army drop-off center on Little River Turnpike in Annandale where I waved off the proffered receipt for the metal cases that were unceremoniously yanked from the trunk and tossed casually onto the pile of surplus flotsam and jetsam that passes for charitable donations in modern America.

"Just one little brown cardboard box between the Phelan pursuit of happiness and bodybuilding in the big house. Fuck going for Olympic gold, Tommy; fix up those broken down units and cut that shitty grass; you've got a business to grow."

I arrived at the office at close to three o'clock and got into a further discussion of the lawn care contract with my dad. I was mighty unhappy with the way the grass on almost all of our projects was looking.

"If that asshole would put more than a pound of seed per acre and used half sharp blades in his mowers, it might look like he – and we – gave at least a little bit of a shit about our residents." I said pointedly.

My Dad was being defensive. "Jimmy's been on him and so have I. I told him that we're the only landlords who were paying on time and if…"

At that juncture, Jimmy burst in and cut into the conversation, " Tommy, sorry for butting in Pat, but John Studley – the guy who sold us the project on Seminary Road – has another one off of Old Lee highway that he wants us to take over."

I snapped, "I thought we'd agreed that we were done buying… at least for now."

"It's only two garden buildings, twenty-two units; Stud says it's clean and would fit right into what we've been buying. He..."

I jumped in with, "I'll bet he says it's perfect for us; no damn conflict there. How much does he want? More important, how much cash will it take? We're damn near out of that shit, you know. "

"He's got the second, and he's under water on it and on the first, too – but not by much – he says. He says it's really good but he needs cash and, against his better judgment, just has to part with it. I made a call to my contact at the bank holding the first – they're holding two of our other notes and love us – we pay. He's certain that they'll go along with this. Studley will be happy to get off for a token, maybe twenty thousand, and the bank will do anything to make sure the project doesn't come back to them. Well?"

I replied, "I doubt that it'll work. We don't have any real cash. You just sprung that broken furnace on me for fifteen thou. I spoke with Money Bags the other day and he says our line of credit with Wells Fargo is down to less than sixty thousand bucks, so it's over with them – forever, or at least until the economy improves. Looks to me like we've got less than forty-five to work with and we'll turn from business people to beggars if we break even a pane of glass someplace.

"Frankly, I don't like it anyway; it's way too close to the edge for FAF. We're now in the top fifteen in property management companies in the region, but we're number one – or last – in exposure. We're too damned leveraged and have to pull in our horns for a while. We've got to be able to show Wells Fargo or Bank of America – or any other source of money - that there's something to FAF beside piles of debt. If we can be cool, we can break into the top ten – or five – in just a few years."

Jimmy said, "You're right as usual – technically, but we're so damn close to hittin' it big, Tommy. If we nail the timing, we could actually be friggin' rich - all of us. Tell him, Pat."

"He's got it, Tom. You've been right every time, and we're leveraged like nobody in the area. Every one percent increase in the value of the projects means tens or even hundreds of thousands to us. We're talking numbers that boggle the mind, and already there's been an uptick in rents around the region. We…"

"Do you guys know how many god damn flaws there are in what you're saying? You say I've been right every time but that this time I'm screwed up. But that's nothing compared to the real stupidity: we're leveraged to where we're so close to being under water that we have to dog paddle our cars into the parking lot, and now you want to push our heads completely under. Jesus, if some old lady's refrigerator goes on the fritz, we're done just like these guys we've been soaking.

"Like I said, by being aggressive we've become one of the top owners and managers of apartments around, and like you guys, I swear I want FAF to move way up on the list – top five, minimum, but we have to catch our breath. We just have to consolidate before we grow again.

"But really guys, give me a break; greed is getting in the way of your judgment."

It was as if what I'd said was in Sanskrit as Jim continued to berate me, "Your Dad's right, Tommy, if we can hang tough for just six months, we won't be FAF, small time jackasses; we'll be major players in the DC real estate market with tens of millions of bucks in equity and under management. We've never had a path to money in our friggin' lives and here with just a little more nerve we could be rich beyond our wildest dreams. You got us to the door, Tommy; now let's bust the damn thing down and go for broke.

"Tell him again, Pat."

My dad said nothing, apparently seeing that this wasn't the time to side with Jimmy.

I was really upset and began to mock them, "Go for broke, I like that; broke is just what we're playing with. Here we line up enough for comfortable futures for all of us – and our kids and theirs, and now greed opens our stupid eyes to the possibility of wealth. Being small time millionaires – ten times what we ever dreamed - no longer cuts it with the FAF management team. Dollar signs are getting in the way of their formerly clear eyesight.

"Come on guys, I say we pull in our horns and play it safe.

"Jesus, Dad, all of your grandkids will be able to go to Duke with what we've got now – if we can just hang in. Why play with matches?"

Dad pleaded with me, "We owe you everything we've got and are lookin' at, Tommy. And, of course our market niche is doing fine. But what's the harm of just looking at the project? We can't lose anything by looking."

Jimmy supported the notion, "Pat's right, Tommy. What can go wrong if we just look the place over?"

"OK, OK, God-damn-it; get me the paper work, and I'll give it a look. But how about you guys get your butts in gear and give the project a real live eyeballing. I'm not taking this on by myself."

"We will; we're on it. You won't be sorry, Tommy. I never liked all those high tech investments; there have been a lot of fortunes made with bricks and mortar, and you broke the code just like a bank robber clicks open the safe," Jimmy said, clearly jumping out of his skin with excitement.

"Tom, the Chamber of Commerce asked me to give the members a quick update at their next meeting on the real estate outlook in Northern Virginia. Could you put together a few talking points for me? I'm up to my ass looking at projects for you," Jimmy said, laughing at me.

"God, you're awful Frawley; I'll do your damn paper. Now just friggin' go; enough with the bullshit...And I never robbed a bank."

Pat and Jimmy laughed and practically ran from the office on their way to see the new miracle project.

Before I could get back to work, Jen was at my door. "Somebody here to see you; you'll never guess who."

"This is supposed to be a real business, and you're the boss, not my damn wife. I'm buried in paperwork; just tell me."

"Amanda Swenson."

"You're shittin' me!"

"In the flesh; and flooding my desk and carpet with her tears."

"What the hell does she want?"

"From what I gather between gasps, she wants to tell you she's sorry for what she did to you."

"I accept her apology, but I'll be goddamned if I'll let her cry all over me. Tell her I forgive her but that I'm too busy to see her now, maybe sometime in the next century."

"You can't do that. You have to meet with her...You do."

"Damn it, you can't play my wife in the office; I'm not...Oh shit, give me a couple of minutes and bring her into Jimmy's office. He's out chasing rainbows."

I was standing behind Jimmy's highly polished partner's desk when she entered. I caught Jen's Cheshire cat smile as she closed the door and vowed to take it up with her when this meeting ended.

For an intolerable period – but probably not more than ten or fifteen seconds – neither of us said a word. Finally I cracked, "Sit down, Amanda. You're looking well. " And there was some truth to it if you ignored her red rimmed and puffy eyes. She retained her fine looks – if you ignored the scarlet blotches - and I had no doubt that on better days she could still wield her powers of persuasion.

She tried to respond but began to weep. Hurrying around the desk and to her side, I placed my hand on her shoulder and handed her a tissue. She looked up and the crimson rivulets were evident; clearly, she had been crying for a long, long time.

"I'm so sorry. I knew it was wrong all along. I've ruined my life and yours. I had no idea that it would end so badly or that it was as serious as it is. I thought…"

I couldn't help myself and blurted out, "It was pretty clear that you guys were talking multiple felonies against the government."

"I know, I know, but somehow the idea that we were doing so much good for the poor people in the villages in Alaska blinded me to the reality…and I was under his thumb.

"The reason I came – beyond asking your forgiveness - was to tell you that I'm separating from Matt and moving away."

I replied, "His case hasn't been resolved, but I understand from a couple of sources that he's trying to plea bargain for something less than fifteen years. It looks to me like the government is going to make it pretty easy for you to split." It was said coldly and cruelly, and I tempered the tone only slightly as my suppressed anger rose.

As I was boring in on her with venom, I noted that I didn't have any difficulty being direct and there was not even the hint of a stammer.

She was clearly trying to pull herself together and get back to the business at hand, "Well I am sorry, terribly sorry, Tommy. I never meant to harm you, even though it's clear now that I should have seen it. Please say that someday you'll be able to forgive me."

I was going to give her a Rhett Butler, `Frankly, my dear, I don't give a damn' but settled for, "I don't harbor any anger toward you, and I believe what you say." I stopped there, refusing to go the distance and offer forgiveness.

"I'm going to New Orleans. As far as the government is concerned, I'm free to relocate and can complete my probation there.

"There was a boy…There is a man I went to college with. He's a physician…divorced. We've been in touch. It's possible that there could be a chance," she babbled into an incoherent silence, weeping on and off as she gained and lost control.

"You didn't have to come. I never cared whether you came, or if you even gave a damn about what happened to me.

"While this has been the worst year of my life, by so damn much you wouldn't believe it, I…"

"I do believe it, and that's why I had to come," she said.

I ignored the interruption and continued. "Despite what I just said, these last months have been among the best and most productive of my life, and I'm certain that my future is brighter despite all those horrible things that happened."

Suddenly, a question that had been in my mind for months arose, "The company you had in Mexico…there was an employee, a woman…was she arrested?"

"Oh, that one; I never knew much about that operation, except what happened to you. I think Matt said she got a job with the company…the big company that was trying to do all that development outside of Cancun."

She returned to her mission with, "That killed me, Tommy. You have to believe that I didn't have anything to do with what happened to you in Cancun."

"I don't care about that," I lied.

"My forgiveness shouldn't matter, but there's no doubt that my anger toward you has eased a lot. I don't even hate Matt any more. I'll never forgive him, but I've wiped his slate clean of my hate. I just want to forget him and the ordeal. That may sound silly, but it means a lot to me. My mental health is a lot better than it's been for a very long time.

"And, believe me, I don't hate you or even bear you very much anger at this point. My future has never looked so good, and I hope that you can make a new start and that `chance' works out for you. As we used to chant so long ago, `Go in Peace.'"

Apparently she heard what she came to hear, or at least enough of it to satisfy the worst of her guilt. She rose and made a slight halting move to what I thought was going to be an embrace but obviously suppressed it and said, "Thanks, Tommy, you were a nice boy and you're a good man.

"If you're ever in New Orleans look me up. I'd love to see you."

She looked into my eyes and smiled. "Good bye, Tommy."

"Good bye, Amanda."

Pulling herself erect, she walked out without turning back.

Jen rushed in. "Well?"

"She's moving out of the area and wanted to clear the air before she left."

"What did she say?"

"She said that she was sorry for hurting me. That was about it. Maybe later at home, after I've had a couple of brews, I'll be able to expand, but right now we've got work to do."

I went back to my office. It took me several minutes to shrug off the encounter and settle down with the books on the project Pat and Jimmy were pushing.

My door opened and Jimmy flew in. "Jen said Amanda was here. Alright, asshole, out with it – all of it. What the hell did she want?"

"She begged my forgiveness and told me that she was benching Mr. Touchdown."

"How'd she look?"

"A nine; I had to deduct a point for her flamed out headlights."

"Her boobs were sagging?"

"No jackass; her eyes were burnt out from crying. Her boobs looked terrific; I checked, but is that all you think about?"

"Wow! Thank you Dr. Phil; like now you're a recovered boob watcher. Come on Phelan, cut the crap, what brought her here?"

"Can't you figure anything? She was answering that old subliminal message that I sent offering to come off the bench for the starting quarterback."

"Bullshit; you never…"

"Of course I didn't; the clock on that one ran out before she got here.

"But I did tell her that you'd be glad to continue as number three on the depth chart and happily attempt a Hail Mary if the new sub wasn't any better than Roby."

"You didn't," he gasped.

"Jimmy, you are one perceptive dude."

"And you're an All American Idiot."

Changing the subject, Jim capitulated, "Pat and I agree; that project Studley's pushing ain't for us. Half the screens are out and there's junk strewn all around the parking lot. It would cost FAF a fortune to put it in minimal shape.

"You were right, and we agreed that we won't question your judgment again."

"At least not till tomorrow," I said with a smirk and continued, "I'd just started on the numbers, and they look as bad as the grounds. Tell Stud, 'No thanks,' and tell your boy at the bank that if they want us to manage it for them after they foreclose, they'll have to come in with enough cash on the front end to bring it up to standard."

At that point, my dad came in, and Jimmy said, "Pat, Tommy agrees that this project is a real dog, and he won't question our judgment again."

Dad laughed and said, "Sorry Tom, Jimmy and I are beginning to see your point on how big FAF should get – at least for now. It looks like our eyes just got a little too big. Maybe we'd be better off being supporting actors to the Rockefellers instead of trying to be bigger than them."

Changing the subject, he smiled and offered, "I know you have your heart set on sending your kids to Duke, but I think they should go to Notre Dame."

"Hell, I don't care if they go to Harvard, but I'm not buying a building to get them in," I said. "You guys saved me a lot of work by seeing the light. How about we call it a day and I spring for the beers? Jen will cover for us."

THIRTY ONE

The routine of my probation proved to be easy; every other week I went to Mr. Jackson's office and found that he, like most government workers, was a time server seeking no trouble. He asked the routine questions about me keeping to the straight and narrow, and I always answered fully, truthfully and positively. We got along by getting along.

On no set schedule but averaging about once every couple of months, Agent Cooper would be waiting for me in Jackson's office to perform his, "Hello, Sunshine," sadism routine. I found it difficult to believe that he could maintain the outlandish level of rage and vitriol for more than two years, but he worked on it like a world class athlete training for the Olympics.

Shortly after my second anniversary of probation passed without great notice from Mr. Jackson, Charles Stetson called me with extraordinary news: Fred Callahan's ill gotten gains from our venture had been found. About as creative as most of the others in our gang, Fred had deposited his trove of Benjamin Franklin etchings in a public storage unit in Manassas.

It seems that after the rental payments on the unit had ceased and become overdue, the security company followed the legal procedures and secured the right to open the unit. As was usual in such cases, they were going to toss the contents into a Prince William County landfill until they found all of the neatly bound portraits of our founding father and called in the police. It was only a matter of days before the alerted FBI agents reverse engineered the project and found that it was my departed partner who had let the rent slip.

According to Charles, despite his spendthrift ways, Callahan was able to put away almost three quarters of a million dollars in his private retirement account in the Manassas Security and Trust unit. The FBI was pretty well convinced that was all that remained of the couple of million that the founder of the gang that wouldn't shoot anybody had not been able to blow in his personal quest to buy the country out of its recession.

I asked if the government had made any other progress at asset recovery, but Charles was unaware of anything on that end, other than that on John Barrow's split. Charles had heard that the widow had turned over John's art collection in final settlement of the Barrow family liability. He added that he had heard that the value of some of the paintings had grown enormously and was likely going to be sufficient to cover far more than John was charged with defrauding from the Corps in the first place.

Charles also said that he'd heard from one of the prosecuting lawyers – completely off the record - that given the value of the settlement, the government was not likely to be overly aggressive in pursuing anything else from Evelyn. Since John had been roped into the scheme much like I'd been, the feds weren't trying to drive her into an early grave by being overzealous in hounding her for more. That, of course, made me feel good.

With that little bit of news, I couldn't wait to discuss the situation with my friend Cooper. But the bastard had disappeared from my life. On my next session with Jackson, I dropped the news about the recovery of Callahan's stash and offered that I couldn't wait to share the news with Cooper.

Jackson smiled and said, "I hate to spoil your fun, Phelan, but I doubt that you'll have that pleasure. A couple of weeks ago, Cooper dropped in and told me that he was putting in his retirement papers and would be gone in a month or so.

"Said he's moving down on Virginia's Northern Neck - Kilmarnock, I think. He bought a place right on the water with a great view and a dock for his boat. Said he's into fishing in a big way."

"No kidding? I never pictured the S.O.B. doing anything but picking the wings off of flies for a hobby; maybe he can use them for bait.

"I've been down there a few times. Some of the older guys I worked with at Belvoir and some of the Corps officers I knew retired to Kilmarnock. I even played golf down there before my troubles; great area.

"Old Cooper's going to have to change his ways though. Screaming and ranting right in people's faces probably won't work too well down there. He'll probably have to come up and visit you in the office to ease his withdrawal symptoms," I said.

Jackson laughed, "You may have a point.

"You're getting to be short timer around here, Phelan, and it's beginning to show. You'd best stifle some of that bull for a while till Cooper or his buddies can't get at you."

Feeling full of myself, I said, "I'm straight as an arrow on my obligations, Mr. Jackson, but somehow old retired farts, no matter how mean they are, living out in the boonies three hours down the road don't scare me at all.

"When this is all over and I feel myself getting complacent, I'm gonna have to drive down to Cooper's place and give him a dose of the old `what for'."

"You better well mind your Ps and Qs for the next few months, and not get too damn full of yourself, or you'll find your butt in a big sling."

"I'll be very careful, Mr. Jackson," I said with a smile.

When I got back in the office, I couldn't wait to get on the internet and spent more than an hour checking real estate sales and property records in and around Kilmarnock. After a difficult search of real estate brokers' sites in both the Northumberland and Lancaster Counties assessors' records, I finally located Cooper's new property on Waterbury Road, way out on Painter Point. What with the price he paid, the waterfront location with unobstructed views across the bay, and the high real estate taxes on the place, it's clear that Cooper had done damn well investing his blueberry money. I couldn't do anything but fantasize on how one day I'd knock on his door and scare the crap out of him. Unfortunately, I had to put it away and deal with real FAF problems.

But I'll be damned if my dreams didn't come true – at least partially - far sooner than I expected. At my very next probation visit, I found Farley Cooper in Mr. Jackson's office acting like a slobbering pit bull just dying to sink his bloody canines into a cringing French Toy Poodle.

Before I could blink, Mr. Jackson begged out saying that he had copies to make and ran out closing the door behind him.

"Surprised to see me, Sunshine?"

"As a matter of fact I am. I heard that you had retired," I said in the most casual tones I could muster.

"You heard almost right; my last day's this Friday. But I didn't want to leave without saying goodbye to you, especially you.

"I want you to know that my hobby in retirement is going to be working on cold cases that are particularly rotten, and yours is at the top of my list...number one, numero uno. I sure didn't want you to think that I would abandon you to agents who couldn't possibly understand just what a sleazebag crook you are. I..."

"I'm sorry Cooper, but didn't you get the word that your theory on my role in the caper is in the friggin' dumpster? It seems that Callahan's share of the money – that you had so generously granted to me – was found right where he stashed it in a storage vault in Manassas."

"Those skittish morons down at the U.S. Attorney's office may have been thrown for a loop by that, Sunshine, but I'm doubling down. There's still maybe half a million bucks out there that Barrow gave you for safekeeping, and deep in my bones, I know that you've got it stashed someplace. You should know that I'm determined..."

For the first time ever, I snapped at him, "Cooper, a long time ago, my lawyer pegged you perfectly; you're nothing but a small time Javert, a half mad, obsessed bully intent on hounding me for the rest of my life. Well just remember that starting Friday you won't have a fucking badge to hide behind. You'll be on your own, just another private citizen of the United States with no more rights – and definitely no more protection - than any other fucking maniac. You damn well better ease up on that phony fucking role of crazy cop in an old French novel."

"That's good, Sunshine, real good, but don't be too quick to try to intimidate me. I'll be on your case with a vengeance starting at the close of business on Friday. You're not going to get rid of me by throwing four letter words around; no way."

I calmed down and spoke with a quiet intensity, "I hear that you've bought a really nice house down on the bay. There's nothing like waterfront property to while away your declining years. It would be tragic if you were to lose it because you overstepped the law in an overzealous pursuit of a person who's paid his debt to society."

For the first time, I saw a look of doubt cross the bastard's face, and his voice sounded far less confident as he cut me off, "You can't scare me. I'll crack you like the rotten egg that you are."

"Waterbury Rd., right? That's a hell of a location – deep water with a dock, eh? I'd have no trouble picturing old Tommy Phelan spending his retirement watching the world go by from that porch. You're a lucky man, Cooper. You're free to pursue any hobby you like, but you have to be careful when your hobby interferes with the rights of your neighbors – or past associates."

"You really are the crooked bastard that I always thought you to be, Phelan. Now I really am going to get you."

"Just saying, Cooper, don't slander me down there; bad things could happen," I was smiling. "By the way, I'm more into golf than fishing, so if you find yourself around some of those fine folks from the Indian Creek Country Club – where I've already played a few times, I'd appreciate if you'd go easy on the defamation. I'd like a clean slate with those nice folks, if your place were ever to fall into my hands."

His rage at my change of demeanor was obvious, and he began to growl and sputter incoherently as the color in his face went way past purple on the maniacal scale.

"I hate to spoil your fun, Cooper, but I'm going out in the waiting room till Mr. Jackson can see me.

"Enjoy your retirement, but watch your back. In these litigious times, there are people just waiting for folks like you to make the smallest mistakes in order to get into their wallets…and onto their porches.

"So, best of luck in Kilmarnock," I said and rose quickly and walked out as he continued to bark out even more threats.

I was certain that I'd struck his most sensitive nerves, and I smiled broadly to him as he barged past me on the way to his car a few minutes later. I felt bad that I swallowed my last line to him; it would have been fun to see him blow a gasket to, `Happy Trails, asshole!'

"What the hell happened while I was making copies?" Mr. Jackson asked when he returned and called me in again.

"Nothing much; I just wished Cooper well in his retirement."

"He looked like you'd punched him."

"I'm sorry you didn't stick around for our parting, but I know how it is when you need copies. I was a long time fed myself and know that you can miss a lot when you just have to get to that copy machine."

We dropped the subject and finished our business. I had to chastise myself for repeated whistling violations on the way back to my office. "Excessive celebration; five yards; repeat first down!"

THIRTY TWO

Jen interrupted me, "A Reverend Knight called. He's the pastor of a Baptist church in Centerville. It seems that a member of his church was at one of those redemption speeches you gave at one of the parishes in Arlington a couple of months ago. He was wondering if you'd consider doing your act at his church."

"Was I that good?"

"It appears that there's a shortage of folks who can sling that redemption hash you've been cooking. It seems that you're making a name for yourself in the salvation business. You're so good at scaring kids away from lives of crime that you've become an ecumenical hero. So cut the baloney; will you do it?"

"Wow; when we quit this racket, you can be my manager and we'll go on the Christian rubber chicken circuit. Alright already, if I'm clear, I'll do it."

"You're clear. Oh, and the good reverend was wondering if you'd buy a table's worth of tickets. It seems that they're a very poor congregation and need that kind of help too."

"What's a table go for?"

"Five hundred for ten plates."

"That's highway robbery. The good reverend's the one who needs redemption. What the hell are they serving?"

"Vulcanized chicken naturally; what did you expect?"

"If it doesn't cover mine, tell him I can't do it."

"Yeah, right."

I laughed. "I thought it was just the Catholics who made me sing for my supper and pay for the mariachi band while I scoffed up the jalapenos and chicken. OK I'll commit for a table, but put the pastor down to write letters to the president and the pardon office when the time comes.

"It's going to take a lot of endorsements to get me that pardon, and even more if you ever expect to see me canonized."

"I've already got him down for a hand written letter describing your ability to walk on water."

"Good girl; it's a start. Hey, tell him to reserve one of those dinners for the rabbi at the nearest temple. I want to be the most ecumenical pardon recipient in history.

"Jen, if it's OK by you, would you ask Jimmy if we could slip the guy an extra five hundred for their local good works. We did that for all the Catholic parishes."

"I know that we're doing fine, Tommy, but given the economic situation, don't you think FAF has been overly generous to these churches and local charities? I mean this, Love; you've redeemed yourself several times over as far as I'm concerned."

"Cast thy bread upon the waters, Jen. You and Jimmy are in charge, but it'll be a while before I feel that I've rid myself of all my guilt."

"Damn you, Tommy! Don't lay your guilt on me like that; I can't take it.

"Jimmy's going to scream, too."

"You can take it," I said with a smile.

THIRTY THREE

I was at sitting at Jimmy's desk when Jen entered with Fred Barrow in tow. "Tom, Fred's here for your two o'clock." With that she turned back and shut the door.

I rose and smiled and offered my hand, "Long time, Fred. How've you been?"

He shook my hand very reluctantly, in the spirit of a man recoiling from touching a leper, and spoke brusquely, "I've been well," with no effort to hide the fact that he was not returning my greeting.

"Have a seat. I've wanted to talk with you for a while, and I'm glad you could make it."

He said nothing as he sat, and I surmised from his frozen face that he hated me. While no words had ever been exchanged, it had been clear for years that Evelyn and he were fully aware that I dealt with my legal predicament by shifting much of the blame to John, and, obviously, they had been hurt by my actions and were still mighty angry.

"For the record, this isn't my office; it belongs to Jim Frawley, one the owners of the company. He and my wife are partners, and they hired me as their accountant and chief cook and bottle washer."

He made no move to interrupt me, so I continued as though I wasn't the least bit upset by his attitude. "Frankly, FAF is doing well, and we're hiring… which is pretty unusual in this day and age. We've added quite a few employees over the past several months, and we're pleased to be doing our bit in reducing the national unemployment statistics," I said with a smile, making an effort to show that I was trying to make a joke.

"Your father was always kind to me, and when our latest opening for a senior property manager and policy analyst came up, I thought of you. John was a mentor to me and spoke many times of our joining forces to create a business. He often said that you were very sharp, and when he was sick and became aware that the plans for his retirement would never work out, he asked me to keep you in mind if I was ever lucky enough to establish a going concern.

"Jim Frawley and my wife have done well with FAF considering the bad economy, and they're looking to expand. The new position is one that calls for real analytic skills as well business talent.

"I asked them for permission to sound you out about the job, and they agreed. I'm sure that we could work a compensation and benefits package that would be very competitive with what you're making as a vice principal in Prince William. Would you be interested in being considered?"

Fred puffed up like rooster. "Phelan, the way you turned on my father after all that he did for you confirmed that there isn't a compensation package in the world that could tempt me to work for any firm with which you are associated.

"My father talked about you all the time and said the most complimentary things. But after he died and was unable to defend himself, you defamed him at every turn to save yourself from having to pull jail time."

I'd thought about this long and hard and wasn't about to take any of his bullshit if the conversation headed this way, "Fred, your father was well aware of how our criminal venture was likely to end. I'm a convicted felon, a thief, and your father was my partner in crime. In fact he helped ensnare me into the gang. He bore a lot of guilt for that and practically told me to do whatever it took to survive what he clearly saw was going to be an unhappy breakup of the scheme. More important, he wanted me to do whatever I could to ease the impact on your mother and you, and I'm trying my damndest right now."

"My father got roped into the situation only because he was blackmailed and threatened with death."

"Right you are. And he joined the others in doing the same damn thing to me. From what I gather, most of the things he did with his share of the gains went to protecting your mother, and I understand that she's doing quite well."

"She is doing very well indeed with no thanks to you, Phelan, and..."

I tried to back down slightly, "I understand how you feel, and my only goal is to try to fulfill the wishes of your dying father. There's a job here at FAF that we're pretty sure you could fill. We'll pay enough to make it worth your while to come aboard, and if you perform the way we think you can, there'll be an ownership stake available."

"Are you deaf, Phelan? Apparently you didn't hear me," he spoke loudly, slowly and clearly, "All the money in the world wouldn't lure me into working with you. Thank you for nothing, and I'd appreciate it if you never contact my mother or me again."

He got up and stormed out without another word.

Jen came rushing in. "How did it go?"

"I tried but he wasn't interested. Period! Give me tons of points for trying and mark the Barrow File...No, make that all the old files, 'Paid in full.'

"It's time for FAF to move on."

The End

ABOUT THE AUTHOR

ray Hearts and Greenbacks is William Brennan's fifth novel. His first three, *A Tattered Coat Upon a Stick*; *Murphy's War*; and *Au Revoir, L'Acadie*, formed a trilogy on the impacts of the great events and issues of the early twentieth century on ethnic neighborhoods of New England's mill cities.

His fourth novel, *Charity for All*, was inspired by a secondary school sex abuse scandal that took place in a small New England town.

The author is a native of Brockton, Massachusetts and a graduate of Boston University. He retired after a thirty-six year career as a public affairs and intergovernmental affairs executive with the federal government. .

He resides in Annandale, Virginia.

www.ingramcontent.com/pod-product-compliance
Lightning Source LLC
Chambersburg PA
CBHW070558130626
46556CB00001B/209